JOE

BE BLESSED!

THE LEGEND OF
JAKE JACKSON

*The Last of the Great Gunfighters
and Comanche Warriors*

WILLIAM H. JOINER, JR.

CONTENTS

*To Gerald Red Elk,
old friend and former
high school classmate*

THE RISE OF SNAKE

If Snake Speck had this figured right, killing Jake Jackson would bring him fame, fortune and respect.

Jackson was well known as the fastest gun on the western frontier. Killing him would make Snake instantly famous. Money would give him the respect of the big ranchers and bankers who now looked down their noses at him. When he passed them on the street, instead of looking the other way, they would now tip their hats and greet him, "Good day, Mr. Speck." Perfumed women would flock to him. He would have a different woman every night if he wanted—maybe two a night.

Snake imagined himself living out of a grand hotel and leaving behind the cold, hard-scrabble camps that he now endured and hated. He hoped he never smelled the smoke from another campfire.

Snake knew Jackson had to be at least sixty years old. Rumor had it that Jackson had slowed down in his old age. Snake was counting on it.

Snake was born in Waco, a small town in central Texas. His real name was Robert Skinner, but his daddy, Ed Skinner, began calling him Snake not long after he was born. Ed took great pride in telling everyone, "Look at my boy! The little peckerhead looks just like a snake!" Whenever someone took a closer look, Ed loved trying to push their face into the crib shouting, "Bite 'em, Snake! Bite 'em!" Ed would then convulse with laughter. The fact that baby Robert was terrified and screamed every time Ed pushed a strange face into his crib was lost on Ed.

Ed Skinner was skinny, with a receding hairline. He had the red bulbous nose and bloodshot eyes of a falling-down drunk. Robert's mother, Maggie Masterson, was a whore. She had frizzy red hair and pasty white skin. Maggie's appearance attracted only the most desperate of men.

Snake had been on his own since he was ten. Ed accidentally shot and killed Maggie because she wasn't making enough money to buy all the whiskey he wanted. Just before he killed her, Ed, who was in a drunken haze, said, "Bitch, I done warned you and warned you 'bout holdin' out on me. Where is the rest of my damn money?"

Maggie begged, "Eddie honey, you know I would never hold out on you. Please calm down."

Ed replied, "Liar!"

When he shot he only intended to crease her ear, to scare her into giving him all the money. But Ed was so drunk that the bullet went through one of Maggie's eyes and blew out a hole in the back of her head big enough that a man could stick his fist in. Ed never figured out that Maggie's earning power had steadily decreased from too many times of being ridden hard and put away wet.

Ed went to the ramshackle old shack that they lived in and told his son that his momma was killed by a thief. "Snake, I got some bad news. Yore poor mamma has done been kilt by some no-count tryin' to rob her."

Young Robert never said a word. He knew it was a lie. Ed told everybody else the same story. He said he found poor Maggie with her brains blown out. No one else in town believed it either, but the only witness was in the graveyard with a tunnel connecting her eye socket and the crater in the back of her head.

No one ever put any flowers on Maggie's grave. The only decoration for her grave was an occasional tumbleweed that blew across the lonely graveyard.

Within a week of killing Maggie, Skinner made the mistake of trying to rob the wrong man and ended up in the graveyard himself with ten bullet holes in him. That night Ed stepped out of a dark alley, grabbed his victim by the arm and stuck the end of his gun barrel in the man's ribs. "Gimme your money and you won't git hurt!"

His victim pretended to pull out his wallet from his inside coat pocket but pulled a pistol instead. The man's first shot knocked Ed to the ground with the force of being hit by a hammer. The shot was at such a close range that it set Ed's shirt on fire. Ed was falling when he managed to pull the trigger on his gun. His shot went harmlessly into the black sky. Ed Skinner was dead before he hit the ground.

His would-be victim said in a rage, "You ain't gittin' my money, but I will give you this!" He emptied his gun into Ed, reloaded and emptied it again just to make sure that Ed got all that was coming to him.

When told of each of his parent's deaths, the ten-year-old Snake never blinked an eye or showed any emotion. The die had been cast.

Snake started saying that his last name was Speck, after a feared outlaw he had heard about. He still went by Snake because he liked to see the fear in someone's eyes when he told them his name.

He didn't want anyone to know that his daddy was Ed Skinner. Snake didn't mind that Ed had a reputation as a thief and a thug, but Ed was also known as a coward and a back-shooter. Snake didn't want folks to think he was yellow too. He soon drifted north, away from Waco and central Texas.

WHITE WOLF

I
t was a well-known fact that Jake Jackson was raised by the Comanche. His Comanche name was White Wolf. His Indian father, Red Elk, was a great war chief.

What Jake learned from being trained as a Comanche warrior by Red Elk gave him an edge in the white man's world. His training taught him to trust his inner senses. Jake could anticipate what was going to happen just by reading a man's face and eyes. His own face and gray eyes were blank, giving nothing away to someone watching him. Doc Holliday once told him, "Jake, if I had your 'poker face,' no one would ever beat me at the card table."

Snake was currently camped in a little grove of live oaks just outside of Weatherford, Texas. The weather over the last month had been cold and rainy. The overcast clouds blocked all light from the stars. Snake shivered as the chilly wind cut through him like a knife. He sometimes felt that he would never be warm again.

He saddled up what loosely could be called a horse and headed into Weatherford. The horse was skin and bones. Snake thought it was stupid to waste money on horse feed.

He told himself that he could get warm in the saloons of Weatherford. Snake was well known enough in Weatherford that most folks would try to avoid him when possible.

Snake had become obsessed with Jake Jackson. He would brag to anyone who would listen, "Jake Jackson ain't shit. I heared all about how fast he is but I can take him. Ain't nobody as fast as me!" Most people prayed for the day that Snake would meet up with Jake.

Snake had been fast enough to take down a laundry list of farmhands, drunken cowboys and washed-up gunfighters, but he was not famous. Instead, he was infamous, known around Weatherford as a bully, a back-shooter, and just plain crazy.

Snake was also a killer, thief and rapist. Even though there was never enough evidence for the law to act, one could always tell Snake's robbery victims by the gunshot holes in their backs. He was the worst kind of psychopath, preferring to rape children—girls and boys. Their pitiful cries did not elicit any sympathy from him. In fact, it only served to spur him on. Slitting their throats when he was through with them was all part of the attraction for Snake. He buried their bodies in remote places where they could not be found. The local community knew only that another child had disappeared.

NED STOWERS

———————————

S nake was careful about who he egged into a gunfight. He only had the courage to confront the obviously inept or those too drunk to have charge of their senses. Snake would goad them into drawing, or in most cases, trying to draw their gun. He picked his targets so carefully that no one had ever fired a shot in his direction.

Snake watched a farm boy push his way through the swinging doors of the Dry Creek Saloon in Tin Top, a little town about ten miles west of Weatherford. Bruce Matney, the owner and bartender at Dry Creek, wished that Snake would get out and stay out of his bar, but he was too afraid of Snake to make an issue of it. Bruce was slightly overweight and had a nervous tic that caused his left eye to twitch.

The farm boy was Ned Stowers. Ned's father had passed away from consumption when Ned was twelve years old, leaving him to run the small, forty-acre farm and to take care of his invalid mother. His mother had been bitten by a diamondback rattlesnake, and the poison had attacked her nervous system, leaving her paralyzed.

Ned's mother was totally dependent on him. He fed her, bathed her and even had to clean her from her bodily functions, changing her home-made diapers. It was natural for a mother to perform those tasks for her child, but totally unnatural for a child to do the same for a parent. At first it was difficult for Ned, but he eventually adjusted to his lot in life as his mother's caretaker. His mother said on many occasions, as tears rolled down her cheeks, "Ned, I'm so sorry I'm such a burden to you. It would have been better if that snake had just killed me."

Ned would always reply as he wiped her tears away, "Now Ma, you just hush up now. I don't mind takin' care of you. I love you, Ma. You and me are all we got." They had no other family to help out.

Ned was wearing a baggy pair of overalls, a straw hat and carrying a small caliber rifle that he used to pot squirrels or the occasional rabbit for a stew. He had black hair like his mother and his skin was deeply tanned from long hours in the sun working the farm. Ned had decided that since today was his sixteenth birthday, he was old enough to drink his first beer. He didn't tell Ma because he knew she would worry about him.

Bruce the bar owner said, "Ned, does your momma know you're in here?" Ned puffed out his chest and replied, "Nope but I'm old enough to do a man's work so I figure I'm old enough to have a man's drink." Bruce noticed Snake eyeing Ned like a copperhead eyeing a rabbit and said, "Ned, you git on outta here. This ain't no place for you. Yore momma needs you." A shiver went up Bruce's spine as he thought he saw Snake's tongue flicker out like a real snake.

Snake smelled blood and interrupted, "Hold on, Bruce. That ain't no way to talk to a full growed man." Snake looked at Ned and continued, "Ain't that right, mister?"

Ned was flattered that someone else besides himself thought he was a man. Ned didn't like the hard look around Snake's eyes but smiled at his new friend and replied, "Thank you, sir."

Bruce cut in, "Now Snake, this boy has to take care of his crippled momma. He's all she's got."

Snake turned toward Bruce. "I figured you knowed better than to butt in my business. I'm only gonna tell you just this once, shut yore mouth!"

Snake said to Ned with a grin, "We don't need no one to tell us how to handle our business, do we, mister?"

Ned began to get a bad feeling in the pit of his stomach as he said, "What business, sir?" Ned suddenly realized that his new friend had an uncanny resemblance to the rattlesnake that had bitten his mother.

Snake laughed, "Well, I need to know iffen you know how to shoot that squirrel gun?"

Ned brightened a little, "Yes sir, I don't mean to brag but I'm a pretty good shot."

Snake responded, "Good, good. See there, that's the kinda stuff I need to know. Now let me ask you this, what's your old lady like in the sack?"

Ned was sure he didn't hear the question right, "I'm sorry sir, I don't understand."

Snake continued his verbal attack, "What the hell is wrong with you boy? You got pig shit in your ears? Who's better? One of those farm girls you probably been dippin', or your momma?"

Bruce pleaded, "Snake..." But he shut up when Snake shot him a murderous look.

Finally, Ned understood and raised his squirrel gun saying, "Mister, nobody..."

That was all Ned got out before Snake blew a big hole in his belly. Ned never even got his little squirrel gun pointed at Snake. Bruce started towards the door. Snake yelled, "Hold it! Where the hell do you think you're goin?"

Bruce said, "I'm gonna fetch the doc."

Snake replied, "The hell you are. You're gonna git your ass back over here and pour me another beer. It was a clear case of self-defense. You heard him say that he knew how to shoot his gun and he was a good shot. I knowed you seen him turn his gun toward me. He, his own self said he was a man. The little son of a bitch got what he deserved tryin' to gun me down."

Bruce handed Snake his beer as Snake grinned wider at Ned and mockingly said, "How you doing boy? Do it hurt much?"

Ned was seated in the floor leaning up against the bar with a hand over the hole in his belly, trying to keep his blood from leaking out. Ned begged, "Wa..ter....."

Snake looked at Bruce, "You heared the man. Git a glass of water!" Bruce handed Snake the water and Snake set it down just out of the reach of Ned. Ned tried to reach the glass but could not raise his hand. Snake sat down in a chair and propped up his feet on a table. He wanted a nice comfortable seat to watch the farm boy die. Snake loved to watch the final light go out in the eyes of his victims. He got a kick out of seeing his victim's face turn blue in death. When Ned's face turned blue, Snake said as he looked at Bruce, "Now ain't that the purdiest shade of blue you ever did see?"

Bruce looked down, choking back the vomit. He was ashamed that he was such a coward.

When word got around about the killing of Ned Stowers, the folks around Tin Top were outraged. The problem was no one was outraged enough to do anything about it.

BIG MAMA

S nake was a coward at heart but no one would oppose
him because he was bat-shit crazy. Most people were
afraid of him primarily because of his total lack of a
moral compass. If you got on Snake's wrong side, you could
find yourself dead in the street after being dry-gulched from
a dark alley.

Snake tracked Jake to the Deadwood Saloon in Ft. Worth.
That wasn't hard to do as Jake hid from no man. The bar in
the saloon was nothing more than a stained ten-foot plank
with the ends nailed to two upright barrels. At the end of
the bar was a cuspidor that contained only a small portion of
the tobacco juice spat at it. The rest of the tobacco quid was
on the sawdust floor around it. There was a big, black, pot-
bellied stove standing in the middle of the floor. The stove
attracted almost as much attention in the wintertime as the
rot-gut whiskey.

There was a slightly warped long mirror hung on the back
wall behind the bar. A picture of a naked woman hung next
to the mirror. Andy Fincher, who owned the bar, told everyone that the woman in the picture was the famous actress
Lillie Langtry, although he really didn't have the slightest idea

who it was. Andy's lie was believable as he had the dark good looks of an actor. It wasn't a stretch for most folks to think he knew Miss Langtry. Some of the men came into the bar just to gaze at the naked Miss Langtry. Many of the men would get through their work days by daydreaming about her likeness. Andy felt like the mirror and picture gave his establishment class.

Andy also employed three "soiled doves:" Kim Becan, Theresa Copeland and Whitney Wiggins. All three women had hearts of gold, which was unusual for those who were in that line of business.

Kim had stringy brown hair and came from a good family from Kansas, but she was tired of living the way she was raised. She longed for a more exciting life. She kept repeating over and over, "That old farm bored me to tears." It was obvious to everyone that she was a little slow mentally.

Theresa had black hair and an oriental look that some of the cowboys and farm hands found appealing. She refused to say where she was from. Most suspected that she had family who would be less than pleased at her career choice. Her main drawback was she was a little bossy. Theresa wasn't much for small talk. Her favorite saying was, "Show me the money."

Whitney was a Texas girl and understood the value of hard work. She was a good earner and Andy finally had to bar her husband Wendell from the saloon, as he kept trying to buy whiskey and charge it to Whitney's account. Whitney told Andy, "As far as I'm concerned, you can throw that bum out.

I work too hard for my money. I damn sure don't want to spend it on that good-for-nothing."

The soiled doves were taken care of by Ettie "Big Mama" Orts. She was a petite woman but earned the name "Big Mama" because she was a little firecracker. Big Mama had a lot of experience taking care of wayward girls. She kept a two-foot iron bar wrapped in twine, then wrapped in tape to enforce the rules. Big Mama named her club Rueben after an old boyfriend who had been mysteriously shot to death in the bed of another whore in another saloon. She could be seen all through the day and night fondly caressing her club and whispering to it as if her long lost lover was still alive.

Big Mama kept the customers from abusing her girls, but more importantly she kept the girls from stealing her money. If Big Mama had to choose between abuse and her money, she always chose the money, saying, "Two can't git on 'em and one can't hurt 'em. They'll be alright." If one of the girls needed to be whacked, Big Mama knew just how to do it so they didn't lose any time on the job.

Big Mama started out each day by telling her girls, "Today is a good day to make money. Today ain't a good day to talk to my Rueben." The girls and the customers quickly learned that it didn't pay to mess with Big Mama.

The whiskey was poured from barrels stored in the back into bottles that were reused time and time again. Few knew that the barrels of whisky had rattlesnake heads in them to give a better flavor. Andy had a homemade still in a shed out behind the saloon to keep the supply of whiskey flowing.

JAKES' GOLD

J ake was dressed for the white man's world. He had found that when he was dressed as an Indian, the white folk panicked, grabbing for guns and screaming. Jake was wearing a black-banded cotton shirt, a black kerchief around his neck, a leather belt, leather boots and a pair of the new riveted, denim jeans made by Levi Strauss. He bought the best clothes and boots that money could buy, not because he was a dandy but because he considered them as tools of his trade. Jake spent so much time on the trail that the "new" wore off of everything in short order. He had his worn-out Stetson with the tie strings pushed back on his head, showing his shock of blond hair, the color of corn silk. If you looked closely, you could see streaks of gray hair intermingled with the blond hair. Jake's twin Colt .45 Peacemakers were in his leather holsters tied down on his leg. His old "scalping knife" was in its buckskin sheath in the small of his back.

Jake also had a hidden cache that contained a breech cloth, a pair of moccasins, and bow and arrows, for when a situation needed a solution to be handled in the Comanche way.

Jake had money in a bank in Ft. Worth and another bank in Dallas. While most folks knew he had some money, he had far more than most people would have believed. The source of Jake's money was a topic of speculation. Most folks figured he got money from folks hiring him to shoot people. No one knew that he had discovered gold in a hidden canyon in the Davis Mountains in West Texas. He had made a deal with the assayer in Ft. Worth to meet him late at night to assay Jake's gold and pay him cash for its value.

Jake also paid the assayer extra for his silence. Of course, it didn't hurt that the assayer was scared to death of Jake as were most people due to Jake's reputation as a gunfighter. Half a dozen trips to the hidden canyon and back secured Jake's financial future.

Even before he had money, Jake never hired his gun out except to collect a bounty for killing or capturing known outlaws. He gave them the chance to surrender, but had no problem killing them if they refused his offer. He used the skills taught to him by Red Elk to live off what the land provided.

Jake also liked having money to help the defenseless and the bullied. Jake hated anything that was one-sided. He liked to even up the odds. He developed this attitude watching his red family lose their land and their lifestyle to the whites. Jake helped anyone he felt was being taken advantage of, whether they were red or white. He would defend a red man against a white man or he would defend a white man against a red man, depending on who he thought was in the right.

SNAKE
SLITHERS IN

T he day Snake found him, Jake was seated in the corner of the saloon with his back to the wall, at a rickety table that had seen its better days. He was always careful to be seated where he was able to see everything and everybody. Jake hated blind spots. Blind spots could get a man killed. Jake was slowly sipping the snake-head whiskey from a shot glass. He knew about the snake heads but he didn't care as he had drank and eaten much worse than that when he lived on the high plains as a Comanche warrior.

Snake took great pains to try to enter the bar without being noticed. He kept his head down, avoiding all eye contact and looking neither left nor right. Snake liked the fact that the bar was full of cigar and cigarette smoke. He thought it helped him hide. Jake spotted him easily as yet another good-for-nothing trying to make a reputation by killing him.

Jake gave a small sigh. He had his fill of killing but he knew that this human coyote would likely try to ambush him and not try to take Jake in a fair fight. If he did face him in a fair fight, Jake would try to talk him out of drawing on him. He always tried to talk his way out of a gunfight, but it rarely worked. He shook his head sadly in remembrance of all the foolish men who seemed like they just couldn't wait to occupy a grave.

Snake stuck his pistol in the front of his pants and closed his coat around it. He wanted to appear unarmed. Snake went to the bar and ordered a beer. He cut his eyes, spying on Jake in the big mirror behind the bar. Snake chuckled and thought to himself, "This big dumb son of a bitch is not gonna know what hit him. I don't know why folks think he's such a big deal. I knowed farm boys that were harder to kill than this stupid bastard."

Snake was turned away from Jake, shielding his actions as he slowly opened his coat and slipped his gun free from his pants. He whirled, cocking his pistol as he prepared to fire at yet another unsuspecting victim as he yelled, "You ain't..."

That was all Snake got out.

This was not Jake's first rodeo. When he came into town, he always slipped the thongs off the hammers of his Colts. His holsters were slick from many years of use. Jake never showed nerves. Some say he had no nerves. The truth was that Red Elk had taught him how to keep his emotions in check, never giving in to nerves or impatience.

As Snake tried his under-handed move, he found something much different than what he was expecting. Instead of a surprised Jake Jackson staring death in the face, Snake briefly saw the business end of one of Jake's Peacemakers belching smoke. Something violently punched Snake in the chest, knocking him back against the bar. As Snake slid down the bar into a sitting position, he wondered why his finger was not responding as he tried to pull the trigger on his gun. He looked down and saw a hole dead center in the middle of his chest. The hole was spurting blood, quickly drenching his shirt. Snake's last thought before he slipped into oblivion was, "What the hell?" Then Snake's face started to fade into his favorite shade of blue.

A cowboy seated at another table, who witnessed the entire incident exclaimed, "Damn! I ain't never seen such as that! Mister, you're faster than a rattlesnake!"

Another cowboy at the table said, "Why hell, no wonder! That's Jake Jackson!"

There was tightness around Jake's mouth as he suppressed his anger at the attempt on his life. He spoke after the gun smoke cleared. "Does anybody know this four-flusher?"

Andy said, "I didn't really know him, but I seen him before. He's Snake Speck. From all I heared about him, I ain't surprised he tried to bushwhack you. I don't reckon folks will miss him much. He was a mean un." The distinctive, pungent smell of gun smoke lingered in the air. It was one of Jake's favorite smells.

Jake flipped a silver dollar to Andy as he walked out. "See that he gets buried. You can have anything you find on him including his gun. He also might have a horse outside." Andy replied with a big grin at his financial windfall, "Whatever you say, Mr. Jackson!"

A cowboy started toward the body to claim his share of the loot but Andy warned him, "Git away from him. Jake Jackson give me his stuff. Iffen you want to do something different than what Jake said, take it up with him. You might be joinin' ol' Snake on the floor!" Another chapter was thus added to the growing legend of Jake Jackson.

Ken Cannon was the grizzled old swamper for the saloon. Even from his youth, Ken was always a few cards shy of a full deck. The whisky had killed off most of the rest of the brain cells from the poor simpleton. Ken used to hang around begging for whiskey until Andy gave him the swamper's job. He got three shots of whiskey a day for mopping the floor and cleaning out the cuspidor.

Ken shuffled over to the mop and muttered to no one in particular, "Iffen I got to clean up all this here blood, I better get more than three damn shots. I better get a whole damn bottle. A body would think that that damn Andy Fincher ain't never seen a nickel before as tight as he squeezes 'em."

Upon hearing of the death of Snake Speck, the folks around Weatherford felt there was no one more deserving of a trip to Hell than Snake. The only regret expressed was that Jake Jackson was such a good shot. Snake's death was too quick. Most felt that he should have suffered the same slow death that many of his victims had endured. But the main feeling that they all shared was relief from being out from under the deadly shadow of Snake Speck.

HELLFIRE

J ake had his fill of being in town. He itched to spend some time on his beloved Llano Estacado, which was named by the Spanish explorer Coronado. It was the home grounds of the Comanche, located in West Texas. Llano Estacado was a featureless sea of grass where even the most knowledgeable Spanish, Mexican or white pioneer could become disoriented, get lost and never be heard from again. When the wind blew—which was practically all the time—the grass moved like waves in an ocean.

Jake now craved that isolation. The sea of grass held no terrors for him as he had spent his boyhood there. It was home. Jake leaped onto the back of Hellfire, his big buckskin stallion, and headed west.

Jake rode Hellfire without the benefit of a saddle or bridle. Jake was in his mid-fifties when he discovered Hellfire. The big stud was running a herd of almost a hundred mares on the far north end of the Llano Estacado. Hellfire had defeated many stallions over the years to accumulate such a large herd of mares. He bore many scars as proof of the fights for herd supremacy. He also added to his harem by raiding ranches and stealing their mares.

Hellfire stood on a bluff overlooking the Dos Chiles Ranchero. The Mexican hacienda was finely built using only the best stone and timber. It was furnished with imported items from Spain and France.

The barns and the corrals were also the best in this part of the country. El Patron for Dos Chiles Ranchero was Diego Garcia. Diego's face had the chiseled qualities of the Spanish aristocracy, down to the pencil-thin moustache. He came from old Spanish nobility and money. Diego bought only the best livestock, taking special pride in his horse herd.

Hellfire watched the vaqueros finish their chores for the day as darkness fell. Hellfire had already stolen some of Diego's prize mares in a previous raid. He had stormed onto the ranch, kicked in the corral and drove the mares back to his home range on the Llano Estacado. Diego's purebred stallion, El Conquistador, which he had imported from Spain, was so incensed that Hellfire was taking his mares that he jumped the fence of his private corral and pursued Hellfire. His intent to kill Hellfire was short-lived as Hellfire kicked El Conquistador to the ground, then sank his teeth in the stallion's royal throat, ending the horse's life.

The next morning at first light, Diego and twenty of his vaqueros rode out to find his stallion and his mares. When they discovered El Conquistador's body, Diego was flushed with anger and shouted, "I will give ten of my best horses to the man who kills the Devil Horse!" The vaqueros were great horsemen and trackers but once they entered the great grass sea, they lost the trail of Hellfire and his new mares. On the ride back to the hacienda, Diego grimly said, "I want this Devil Horse shot on sight!"

Hellfire watched from the bluff. He waited until after midnight, when every light on the ranch had gone out, and then he slipped down to the corrals. He was careful to be quiet and to stay out of sight. In his first raid, he ran over and kicked over everything that was in his way. This time was different. As he sidled up to and eyed the corral gate, Hellfire figured out how to open it. He quietly unlatched the gate and silently drove the mares out at a walk. The next morning the ranch woke up to an empty corral. No one had heard a thing. None of the vaqueros could remember El Patron curse so long and so loudly.

Jake had watched Hellfire for over a year until the desire to ride the big buckskin was overpowering. Jake moved in and joined the wild horse herd, becoming a horse himself. He moved when the herd moved and stopped when the herd stopped. At first Hellfire was having none of it. He charged Jake repeatedly, intending to kill him, but Jake had a way of engaging Hellfire's eyes that reassured the horse that the man meant no harm. The other horses came to accept him as one of them. Jake could walk freely among the herd without any of the horses being disturbed.

To say that Jake had tamed Hellfire was not accurate. No one could tame Hellfire. Their relationship was more than that. Finally one day, Hellfire came up to Jake to smell his extended hand. Jake spoke to him in Comanche and in English, switching back and forth between the two:"Easy tami, little brother. I will never hurt you. I want you as my friend."

Gradually over a period of months, Hellfire would allow Jake to climb on his back and ride him without saddle or bridle. Eventually, Jake could communicate with the horse with his legs, knees and most importantly, with the meshing of their minds. Hellfire knew what Jake wanted. The horse chose to please the man.

It thrilled Comanche and white men alike to see Jake ride Hellfire without a saddle or bridle. The big buckskin stallion became as famous as Jake himself. Every year Jake would ride Hellfire back to the great grass sea during breeding season. Hellfire would find his mares, run off all the pretenders to his throne, and service what was his. When Jake returned in a few months, Hellfire would gallop to greet him. The horse went eagerly with the man because they both loved to be in each other's presence.

Hellfire was also theft-proof, as a couple of dumb-ass cowboys, Wendell Wiggins and Bob "Smiley" Wiley, discovered when they tried to steal him. Wendell and Smiley had reputations as being loafers and having an aversion to anything resembling work.

It had been years since Smiley had seen his wife, Annie. She finally had enough of his laziness and escorted him off the family farm using a skillet as a persuader. It took several months before all traces of the knots she put on his head were gone.

Wendell told Smiley, "I'm telling ya, we get our hands on this horse, we won't ever have to work or worry about money agin. We can just take him around and put on shows. We're gonna be rich!"

Hellfire was also a great watchdog, snorting when he sensed an intruder. One night as Jake dozed by a dying campfire with his hat over his face, the two horse thieves approached. He heard Hellfire give a soft snort. If the two saddle tramps could have seen his concealed face, they would have wondered why Jake was grinning.

Jake never tied up Hellfire. The horse was free to come and go as he pleased. When they got within ten yards of their target, Hellfire bared his teeth, flattened his ears and charged them. As they took off running, Bob screamed, "That ain't no horse, that's the Devil hisself!"

Wendell shouted back, "Yeeooww! Shut up and run! He just bit a big piece out of my ass!"

They managed to get back to their horses and ride off, but left behind several large chunks of their clothes and hide. They could hear Jake's deep belly laughs as they barely escaped with their lives. If the bites from Hellfire weren't enough, their mad dash to escape in the black night took them through several mesquite thickets. The mesquite thorns left them scratched from head to foot. The next morning they looked like they had lost a fight with a mountain lion.

HENRY AND MARTHA

H enry and Martha Jackson had tried to make a go of a small farm in Arkansas. They had emigrated from England. The couple had used the last of their savings traveling to Arkansas and buying the small 80-acre farm.

Henry was a tall, muscular Englishman with blond hair and gray eyes, who did not fear any man or hard work. Martha was a classic daughter of Scotland, with bright red hair and dancing blue eyes. Even as a child, Martha was always an adventurous soul. After marrying Henry, none of her family were surprised that she was excited about packing up and moving to the Promised Land: America.

Not long after building a small, crude log cabin with a dirt floor, Martha gave birth to their first child, a robust boy with blond hair and gray eyes. As Martha looked at the new baby, she told Henry, "Darling, he's you made over!" When Henry first held Jake, his eyes glistened with pride at such a fine son.

There wasn't much that Henry Jackson couldn't do, with the exception of one thing. He couldn't make it rain. A draught destroyed Henry's corn crop not long after the green shoots first stuck their heads out of the black dirt. With the passing of each day, searching the sky for even the smallest of clouds, Henry's and Martha's hopes sank lower and lower.

Finally, Henry knew it was time to face the truth. He told Martha something that she already knew. "Martha, this farm is not going to make it."

Martha put a comforting arm around him and soothingly said, "I know, honey. It's not your fault. No man could have done more than you have."

Later that night as the fire in the fireplace died down and Martha nursed the baby, Henry softly said, "Martha, I think we should sell this farm and get whatever we can. I hear that there is prime farm land for the taking in Texas. When we were in town the other day, there was a poster that said there was a wagon train leaving Ft. Smith heading to Texas."

Martha replied, "Honey, I don't care where we go, as long as we're together."

After selling the farm and using the money to buy a prairie schooner, stocking it with supplies and provisions, the Jacksons struck out for Texas, one of twenty wagons on the wagon train. When the train was out of Arkansas and well into Texas, one of the wheels on the Jackson wagon broke down. Henry had had enough foresight to pack an extra wheel. As the other wagons pulled around his, everyone offered to help, but Henry told each one, "It's not necessary. I will change this wheel out and catch back up in no time."

Martha watched the wagon train disappear over the next ridge. She had an uneasy feeling about being left alone. Henry wrestled the spare wheel out of the wagon and began the task of replacing the broken one.

Red Elk and the rest of his war party of ten warriors silently watched from the concealment of the heavy brush inside the tree line. With the bright sunshine and cloudless blue sky, the Indians were careful to stay deep in the shadows. Each of the warriors wore breechcloths and moccasins. All of their faces were painted. Red Elk had half of his face painted white and the other half painted black. The rest of the warriors had their faces painted in various colors of red and yellow, but all had some black on their faces as black was the color of war. They were armed to the teeth with bows, arrows, knives, toma-hawks and lances.

Red Elk was the largest man in his tribe. He was tall and broad, and took great pride in his hair. It was long and recent-ly greased, parted in the middle with the part painted red. It was braided with leather thongs tied around each of the twin braids. There was also a slender braid at the top of his head called a scalp lock.

When Red Elk figured the wagon train was well out of earshot, he nodded his head to the two warriors who already had arrows notched. The first inkling Henry had that there was Indians around were the two arrows thudding into his body, one in the upper chest and one in the thigh of his right leg.

The air was suddenly filled with blood-curdling war cries. Henry's gun, a Navy Colt, was stashed in the wagon out of reach. His only weapon was a three foot iron bar that he was using to change the wheel. Six of the warriors attacked Henry, all eager to collect his scalp as a trophy to impress the Comanche women. As he was swarmed by the Indians, Henry was not afraid for himself but he was terrified about the welfare of Martha and baby Jake.

Henry fought like a man possessed. He crushed the skull of Soaring Eagle by swinging the iron bar like a hammer. Pieces of Soaring Eagle's gray brain matter splattered up against the wagon. Henry then impaled Many Coyotes with the pointed end of the bar, driving it through his sternum with the end of the bar protruding from his back. Many Coyotes dropped to his knees and toppled over as blood gurgled from his mouth. Henry managed to wrestle away Howling Wolf's knife from him and slash his throat so severely that Howling Wolf was almost beheaded. His head barely stayed attached by a thin layer of skin on his neck. The other three warriors took Henry to the ground, slashing and hacking at him. Henry finally went limp as his life's blood drained out of his many wounds from arrows, knives, lances and tomahawks.

As Wild Goose pulled back Henry's hair and started to take his scalp, Red Elk barked out, "No! This was a great warrior! We will not take his hair!" Neither Red Elk nor any of his warriors had ever seen a white man fight and die like this. All the white men that had died under Red Elk's knife had cried and begged for their lives. The Comanche would sing songs around their campfires for many years about the brave death of this great white warrior.

When the Comanche attacked, Martha had quickly put the baby inside the wagon. She armed herself with a butcher's knife and stood between little Jake and the Indians with a fierce look of defiance on her face. The Indians marveled at the white woman's courage. The white women they had seen facing death were hysterical and begging. Some even defecated and urinated on themselves from fear. Martha had just witnessed her beloved Henry's death and was determined she would go to her death defending little Jake. Martha crouched with her knife pointing at them and hissed, "Come on you red bastards, just try to get my baby!"

Normally, when Comanche raided Spanish, Mexicans or whites, they killed all the adults and children who couldn't keep up. The women were gang raped and killed when their usefulness was done. The children who could keep up were taken hostage and eventually sold to slave traders.

To some whites, the Indians were nothing more than sub-human savages, needing to be eradicated like so many coyotes or cockroaches. Most whites had heard that the only good Indian was a dead Indian. But for the whites to claim the high moral ground was laughable. The European countries where most of the whites had emigrated had long histories of torture, including disembowelment, impalement, burning people alive, and flaying or skinning people alive. White men also committed atrocities on defenseless Indian women and children, such as the massacre at Wounded Knee, South

Dakota. Indians could be cruel and merciless, but no more so than the whites.

Red Elk approached Martha and without warning, plunged his lance through her heart, killing her instantly. This swift and painless death was the ultimate compliment from a Comanche. He continued on to the wagon. After determining that the baby was a boy, Red Elk gathered Jake up to take him to their village to give to his wife, Prairie Flower. If the baby had been a girl, one of the braves would have grabbed her by the ankles and bashed her head in against the side of the wagon. Boys were valued much more than girls in Comanche society.

Red Elk and Prairie Flower had lost a baby boy Red Elk had named Golden Eagle, to pneumonia several months before. Prairie Flower was still in deep mourning for Golden Eagle. Red Elk could see that she could not shake her sadness. Even though Prairie Flower was still beautiful, he hoped this white baby would bring her back to be the joyful, cheerful woman who he loved.

The warriors pilfered the Jackson's belongings in the wagon. One of the warriors, Ten Bears, found their Bible. He knew it was a sacred book to the whites. Ten Bears was thin but was as tough as a buffalo hide. He had a hawk-like face and was acknowledged as one of the best thinkers in the band. Ten Bears took the book, hoping that the Great Spirit would bless the tribe because they now possessed it. Ten Bears was also the tribe's medicine man.

Once they had everything they wanted, they set the wagon and the remaining belongings on fire. Red Elk said, "It is time to return to our village." The surviving warriors began shrieking war hoops of victory as they galloped away.

The wagon master was old Gus Thomas. He was a retired U.S. Calvary sergeant. Gus had a little bit of a pot belly but was still strong as an ox. He had led several wagon trains from Arkansas to Texas. Gus was the first to notice the smoke.

He shouted, "Circle the wagons!" As the wagons started to circle, Gus then pointed to five other men that were also mounted. "Follow me!" he yelled as he galloped toward the smoke. As he and his men got closer, they slowed down, not wanting to stumble into any Indians until they were ready for them, but the Comanche were already miles away. When Gus saw the Jacksons' bodies, he cursed, "Damn it all to hell!"

Two of the men got down and began the sad task of burying Henry and Martha. Gus and the rest of the men cast a wary eye watching for the return of the Indians. While they tied two sticks together to form a cross for each grave, Gus knew that the markers would eventually fall over. The grass would cover the graves, the fallen markers leaving no trace of the two pilgrims. But Martha had gotten her wish. She and Henry would always be together.

THE NUMINU

T he Comanche are a Plains Indian tribe. Their territory consisted of what is now eastern New Mexico, southeastern Colorado, southwestern Kansas, western Oklahoma and northwest Texas. They were the dominant tribe on the southern Plains. The Comanche numbered tens of thousands at one time. To this day there is still a large population of Comanche in and around Lawton, Oklahoma.

The Comanche called themselves Numinu, *The People*. In the 1700s they joined with the Shoshone but eventually split off into twelve bands. They were basically hunter-gathers. The advent of the horse in their lives made the Comanche much more proficient at everything. The Comanche became perhaps the greatest horsemen that had ever lived, rivaled only by the Cossacks who lived on the grassy steppes of Russia, a land very similar to the Llano Estacado. The Cossacks and the Comanche were on horseback as soon as they could walk. The horse caused the Comanche to drastically change their lifestyle as they could now hunt and fight far more efficiently.

The Comanche were nomadic, moving frequently in search of buffalo. They lived in tipis, structures that were supported by wooden poles covered with buffalo hides. The entire camp could be packed and ready to move in less than half an hour. The Comanche's diet consisted of fruits, nuts, wild-root vegetables and meat. Each band was ruled by a tribal council usually consisting of the wisest and most proven warriors. The Comanche bed was a buffalo hide suspended from four poles forming a small hammock.

When the returning raiding party came in sight of the village, a great clamor and excitement spread as *The People* rushed to see what plunder had been brought back. The shouts of jubilation turned to wailing and keening when the horses draped with the three bodies of Soaring Eagle, Many Coyotes and Howling Wolf came into view. In grief, the mourners slashed their arms with knives. These three men had fathers, mothers, wives, sons and daughters. All were grief stricken at their deaths.

Prairie Flower ran to Red Elk when she saw that he carried a small bundle in his arms. Red Elk leaned down from his horse as he handed little Jake to her and said, "Meet your son." Satisfaction flooded Red Elk's spirit as he saw the first genuine smile from Prairie Flower in months. She quickly took her new son to their tipi to begin pampering and tending to him.

Red Elk later named his new son White Wolf.

Children were a great gift to the Comanche. Every night around the campfire, the warriors, and sometimes the women, told stories. The children begged for stories every night. They loved to hear even the old stories that they had heard many times. Young and old agreed that Ten Bears told the best stories. He used a different voice for every character in his stories.

"We want Big Cannibal Owl! We want Big Cannibal Owl!" chanted the children. Even though they had heard the story many times, the children always wanted to hear it again. Big Cannibal Owl was reputed to live in a cave in the Wichita Mountains. He would come out at night to eat bad and disobedient children.

Ten Bears began the story. "Big Cannibal Owl loves to eat bad children. He has grown fat eating bad children." Ten Bears then waddled around the campfire with his belly pooched out. imitating the monster owl. Ten Bears continued, "Do we have any bad children here?" as he looked at each child. Ten Bears cocked his head as if he just heard something. "Wait… what was that…?" Everyone knew what was coming next. One of the grandfathers or grandmothers would pull a buffalo hide over their heads and run screeching into the light of the campfire. The children would scream and run to their tipis as the adults laughed heartily. They would come back in a few minutes laughing and giggling. Everyone knew that the buffalo-hide monster owl would come, but all the children were still scared. The truth was some of the adults were a little scared, too.

There was one person in the tribe that Ten Bears could not scare. It was his woman, Kicking Squaw. While Ten Bears was rail thin, Kicking Squaw weighed more than the combined weight of any other two members of the tribe, man or woman. Kicking Squaw usually got her way, either with her sharp tongue or at night under the buffalo robes. Ten Bears was afraid of no man and had proven his courage and fear-lessness many times in battle, but Kicking Squaw could make him visibly flinch whenever she screeched, "Ten Bears!"

The other warriors made no comments about Kicking Squaw because they did not want her focus to be on them. The other women could not conceal their smiles and snickers when their brave warriors went the other way when they saw Kicking Squaw coming.

The only offspring from the union from Ten Bears and Kicking Squaw was a girl, Cat's Paw. Cat's Paw was a beauti-ful child, resembling neither Ten Bears nor Kicking Squaw. She had a spirit that set her apart from the other Comanche girls. Kicking Squaw made her a buckskin dress as soon as she could walk. Most days her little dress could be found any place in the village wherever Cat's Paw had removed it to run free and unencumbered by any clothing restraint. This prac-tice continued until Cat's Paw turned five years of age and modesty finally prevailed.

She was also unlike most Comanche girls in that she said whatever was on her mind. The other women and even the warriors were reluctant to discipline her because they did not want to incur the wrath of Kicking Squaw, who doted on her daughter. While she could be a source of aggravation to others in the village, most agreed that Cat's Paw was destined to be the wife of a great chief.

When Comanche girls were old enough to walk, they fol-lowed their mothers, big sisters, aunts and grandmothers, learning to cook, make clothes and do the many chores that were the lot of Comanche women. Traditionally, girls wore buckskin dresses as soon as they were old enough to walk.

White Wolf enjoyed a different lifestyle than girls or women of the tribe. He was an expert horseman by the age of 6 and a skilled archer by the age of 8. Red Elk also taught him the history of the Comanche. White Wolf soon became an expert hunter. He hunted with the other boys and they were allowed to range as far from the village as they wanted. The bonds that he developed with his Indian brothers as boys would serve them well in their later lives as men.

As a young boy, White Wolf shunned clothes as he preferred to be naked. When he got older, he eventually wore a breechcloth.

White Wolf and the other boys were held in high regard among the tribe. Each member of the tribe knew that the men and even the boys might be required to lay down their lives for *The People*. At nine years of age, White Wolf killed his first buffalo, and Red Elk, with great pride and celebration, honored him with a feast. Around the campfire that night in the midst of the celebration, White Wolf was called upon by many members of the tribe to tell the story of the hunt and the kill. All had heard the story about White Wolf's incredible kill, but they wanted to hear it from him.

White Wolf said, "I was riding my brave pony, Runs Like the Wind. I rode up next to the big bull and shot three arrows into him." White Wolf pantomimed shooting three arrows, then continued. "My pony stepped in a hole and as he went down, he threw me over his head." All knew that it must have been a violent fall for an expert rider like White Wolf to be thrown. White Wolf then said, "I lost my bow during the fall. When I stood up, the wounded bull was only a few feet from me. He charged, and there was nothing for me to hide behind. I managed to dodge him and leapt on his back as he went by me."

At that, Red Duck began whooping, saying, "I saw White Wolf ride the buffalo and kill him." The rest of the tribe joined in with shouts celebrating the buffalo ride and calling White Wolf a great hunter.

When the noise had died down, White Wolf continued, "I took my knife and began stabbing him. When the bull had lost enough blood, he slowed down and finally came to a stop. I then cut his throat. When he went to the ground, I cut out his heart. I ate part and shared the rest with my brothers." The shouts and whoops that followed were ear splitting.

White Wolf's story was told around many campfires down through the years as the greatest buffalo kill ever. No other warrior had ever ridden a buffalo and killed it with just a knife. Over a period of time several boys, in an attempt to gain glory, tried to duplicate the feat of White Wolf. Each attempt resulted in their deaths, as the buffalo always won.

The Comanche had no set meal time. They ate whenever they were hungry. It was not formal as they would use a pointed stick to spear whatever was available from the cooking kettle. Usually they stood while they ate. A special treat was enjoyed when a buffalo calf was killed. Its stomach was slit open and the sweet milky contents were scooped out to be handed out to the children.

QUANAH

The summer of White Wolf's tenth year saw his band, known as the Buffalo Eaters, join with another band, the Travelers. Peta Nocona was the chief of the Travelers. Nocona's father was the great chief Iron Jacket, known for wearing a Spanish coat of mail. Some said that Iron Jacket could blow bullets away with his breath. Nocona had a white wife, a captive. Her name was Cynthia Ann Parker. They had a son who was the same age as White Wolf, named Quanah.

White Wolf became best friends with Quanah. They immediately had something in common. They both had white blood and gray eyes. White Wolf did not know that Quanah Parker was destined for greatness. Quanah would become the greatest of the Comanche chiefs. He prevailed against the might of the U.S. Army, never losing a battle to the army's superior numbers and firepower. The U.S. government eventually overcame the Comanche not just with military might but also with economic weapons. Their encouragement of commercial buffalo hunting reduced the millions of buffalo to just a few thousand. The Comanche were dependent on the buffalo, not just as a source of meat, but because they utilized every part of the animal to make everything from clothes to water bags to bowstrings. Quanah eventually surrendered his tribe as he had to choose between the white man's way or the annihilation of the Comanche.

White Wolf and Quanah were superior to other boys their age in every way. They were physically stronger, better horsemen and more skilled with the bow and arrow. Most of the time the two boys rode off to hunt as a pair.

The boys were twelve when on a hunt they spotted a buck deer. They ,slipped off the backs of their horses without making a sound tied them and began the stalk. The boys stuck to the shadows. The cloudless sky was a brilliant blue with the yellow sun beating down. White Wolf whispered to Quanah, "Be quiet, little brother."

Quanah whispered back in White Wolf's ear, "You're the one who needs to be quiet instead of crashing through the forest like a drunken buffalo. And quit calling me little. I'm bigger than you."

White Wolf grinned as he went to the left of the deer as Quanah went to the right. They were moving just inches at a time when they were startled by an arrow slamming into the deer, knocking it off its feet. It kicked a few times and died. An Apache broke his concealment and came striding to his kill. A second Apache trotted over as they begin to quickly skin and quarter the deer.

The Apaches and the Comanche were deadly enemies. A Comanche warrior was greatly praised and exalted when he brought in an Apache scalp or Apache ponies. Even though both boys were motionless and had not made a sound, the keen eyes of one of the Apaches spotted them.

After muttering something to alert the other Apache, both warriors charged the boys, screaming war cries and threats. The first Apache ran toward White Wolf shouting, "I will skin you, then cook and eat you!" White Wolf and Quanah had already notched arrows in their bows in anticipation of taking down the buck. With nowhere to run and no time to run, the young Comanche drew back the strings of their bows and waited for the Apaches to get within range of their arrows. Sweat began to drip from their foreheads into their eyes. Both boys blinked rapidly to clear their vision. The Apaches had pulled their knives and were ready to plunge them into the hearts of these two hated Comanche spawn.

White Wolf and Quanah released their arrows simultaneously. Each arrow found its mark, deep in the Apaches' hearts. Absorbing the shock of the arrows slowed down the attackers but they still kept coming. The Apache who had singled out White Wolf screamed, "I will cook and eat your dog of a mother!" The boys quickly notched another arrow and sent it on its way, another heart shot. Both Apaches staggered from this volley but somehow recovered and continued toward the boys at a slower pace.

Two arrowheads in the heart would knock down and kill most men. But the American Plains Indians were made of sterner stuff. Their environment was harsh, requiring people with sturdy constitutions. An issue that would derail a white man would be business as usual for an Indian.

The killing shots were the third arrows, this time through each Apache's throats. One dead Apache fell with his head five feet from Quanah's feet. The second Apache's body knocked over White Wolf. The Apache warrior breathed his last breath as he lay on top of White Wolf. White Wolf had to actually wiggle out from under the large dead Apache.

The boys stood on shaky legs, their hearts pounding and trembling from the excitement and the terror of near death. The smell of the two Apaches caused their noses to wrinkle in disgust. When they had calmed down somewhat, White Wolf said, "My Apache was much harder to kill and is bigger than yours!"

Quanah responded, "You are crazy, White Wolf. My Apache is far bigger than yours. I think that thing that you killed with your lucky shots may be a squaw!" Both boys laughed out loud until Quanah said, "We need to be quiet because these two were not by themselves. They have to be part of a war party." Both boys kicked the carcasses and continued to quietly mutter insults to the dead Apaches.

The boys then quickly cut the scalps of the Apaches from their skulls and took them as trophies. They quickly located the Apaches' horses and galloped back to the village, carrying the bloody scalps and dragging the captured horses behind. White Wolf and Quanah galloped through the village from one end to the other, screaming their war cries, causing children, women and even warriors to scatter to avoid being ridden over. As the boys hoisted the scalps, the entire village added their voices with their own war cries and shouts of jubilation. The crescendo of noise was deafening.

HUNT FOR
THE APACHE

Finally Red Elk said, "We are proud of you boys, but you must now take us to where you found the Apache dogs. There will be more in their war party. We must find them and kill them as soon as we can." The warriors quickly mounted and rode out of camp, whooping. They didn't go far before becoming silent. They did not want the remaining Apaches warned.

White Wolf and Quanah swelled with pride when the war party came to the scalped, arrow-filled bodies of the two dead Apaches. Ten Bears quickly picked up the trail made by the Apaches and began back-trailing them. Ten Bears went ahead as the war party cautiously followed. After traveling about five miles, Ten Bears held up his hand for the silent war party to stop. He slipped off his horse and crept forward on foot. In about an hour, he returned just after the sun went down. The old wives tale many settlers had heard that an Indian would not fight after dark has cost the lives of a number of ignorant whites and Mexicans.

Ten Bears quietly said to Red Elk, "There are seventeen of the Apache dogs camped on the other side of that far ridge." Red Elk replied in a voice just above a whisper, "We will surround them on foot and kill this threat to *The People*. We will teach the Apache that there is a price to pay to come into our territory."

The warriors dismounted and gathered around Red Elk. He gave each an individual role to play in the attack. When he got to White Wolf and Quanah, he said, "You two will stay here and guard the horses." As Red Elk expected, the boys were livid with rage. White Wolf started to protest but a stern look from Red Elk caused him to shut his mouth.

Once all of the Comanche warriors had snuck into place, Red Elk gave the call of the whippoorwill to signal the attack. The Apaches also heard the bird call. They knew immediately that it was a Comanche signal but it was too late. The night air was filled with Comanche arrows finding Apache targets. Comanche war whoops were intermingled with Apache war cries. The Comanche warriors poured into the enemy camp. Five of the Apaches were dead instantly from the first round of arrows. Three more were badly wounded. The nine healthy Apaches fought with a fierce desperation, eyes hard and jaws set.

Death was preferable to being taken captive by the enemy. Whether it was Apaches taken captive by the Comanche or the Comanche taken captive by the Apaches, it ended up the same. The captives were in for a cruel and prolonged death. One by one the outnumbered Apaches were cut down. When the fighting ended, fifteen of the Apaches were dead and the remaining two had been overpowered and captured. The captives had their arms and legs bound with buckskin cords. Each captive was slung over the back of a horse, his hands and feet tied together under the horse's belly. The dead were scalped and their hair tied to war lances.

The Comanche had suffered the loss of two of their warriors, Sturdy Oak and Eagle Hunter. In spite of their deaths, this was a great victory for the Comanche. The fallen warriors were tied on the backs of two horses, to be taken back to the village for an honorable burial.

The Apaches had twenty horses in their remuda. The Comanche warriors mounted the Apache horses and rode back to where White Wolf and Quanah were holding and watching their horses. White Wolf and Quanah turned the Comanche horses loose as they mounted, and the entire party started back to the village. The loose Comanche horses followed the war party.

When the war party got within hearing distance of the village, the warriors began shrieking their war whoops. The entire village was waiting and joined in the loud celebration. The captives were tied to a stake in the middle of the village and were poked with sharp sticks throughout the night by the women and children. One old woman, Star Dancer, said with great satisfaction, "You Apache dogs killed my son, Eagle Hunter. Now, you must pay!" She took a sharp stick and poked out one eye from each captive. Star Dancer grunted,

"I will leave you with one good eye so you will be able to see what *The People* will do to you."

Another old crone, Falling Rain, whacked off the ears of the captives and threw them to the dogs to eat. She laughed at them. "You can still hear without your ears. When you are almost dead, we will dig you out of the pit and I will cut off your little worms and balls. The dogs will feast on them!"

A large bonfire was built. There was dancing and many songs were sung praising the victorious warriors. There was also keening and mourning for the loss of Sturdy Oak and Eagle Hunter.

White Wolf and Quanah were now being treated with even more respect. The boys were very aware of their newfound status and began to carry themselves with more dignity. They had never felt more proud than when they were called upon to tell of the killing of the first two Apaches. Each boy told his story with an eye to one-up the other.

White Wolf stood and said, "The Apache who I killed recognized me as the more dangerous enemy. He knew if he could kill me, my brother would be at their mercy. I was fighting for both of our lives. The Great Spirit was with me and I was able to save us."

Quanah danced around the fire saying, "I love my brother. I know it is my duty to protect him. I was glad when the Apache warrior attacked me and the Apache squaw chose him. It was a great victory for both of us."

The entire village laughed as all were familiar with the friendly rivalry between the two.

At dawn the next morning, two large holes were dug, big enough to bury each captive with just his head above ground. Ten Bears took his scalping knife and cut away their eyelids so the Apaches could not close their eyes. Then he sliced off both scalps, lifting the bloody patches of hair high in the air as he and the entire tribe screamed war cries and insults to the Apaches.

The prisoners took three days to die. All the male Comanche, when needing to relieve themselves, would urinate on the heads of the Apaches. The urine caused their eyes to sting, adding to their misery and humiliation. Falling Rain made good on her promise. With their last breaths, the Apaches were dug up. While they were still living, the crone sawed off their genitalia and fed it to the dogs.

VISION QUEST

A t the age of 14, White Wolf was ready for his vision quest. This was the rite of passage from boyhood to manhood, the most important time in a Comanche boy's life. As the medicine man, Ten Bears gave White Wolf a buffalo robe, a bone pipe, tobacco and material for building a fire.

White Wolf would fast for four days, waiting for the visit from his guardian spirit. A boy seeking his vision was left at a special place, such as a significant warrior's grave. Usually, this was within a half a day's ride from the village. But Ten Bears and White Wolf rode hard for two days before reaching the place where Ten Bears left him and returned to the village.

White Wolf built a fire and dozed fitfully during the four days. The second day saw a light rain begin to fall. White Wolf pulled his buffalo robe over his head and waited it out. He had smoked all of his tobacco by the third day. White Wolf prayed to the Great Spirit to send him his vision.

On the fourth day of fasting, White Wolf received his vision. There were two images in the vision. One was a great white wolf. The second was a tall white man with blond hair and gray eyes. White Wolf did not know what to think of the white man.

When White Wolf rode back to his village, he sat down in Red Elk's tipi to share his pipe and counsel with Red Elk and Ten Bears about his vision. For a while they passed the pipe, enjoying the smoking of the tobacco. After a nod from Red Elk, White Wolf said, "My vision had a great white wolf, but it also had a white man who had my color of hair and eyes. I am troubled by this. I don't understand who the white man is."

Red Elk replied, "The white man in your dream was a mighty warrior. He is the great white warrior that we sing about around our campfires. He is your white father."

Ten Bears added, "The place where you searched for your vision was the gravesite of your white father and white mother."

Ten Bears handed White Wolf the Bible that he had kept hidden for fourteen years. "This is a sacred book owned by your white father and mother." Later in life, White Wolf wanted to know what the words on the papers meant. When he began learning to read the white man's words, he also discovered that his father's and his mother's names were listed in the front of the Bible as well as a genealogy of his white family.

White Wolf now knew that his white father and mother had been killed by Red Elk, Ten Bears and the Comanche warriors. He had always felt that his red family was his true family despite the fact that he knew he was white. Comanche cared little about the color of one's skin as long as the person proved themselves worthy of being a member of the tribe. How White Wolf felt towards his red family did not change with the new information. He understood the Comanche way and accepted it.

THE WHITE
COMANCHE
WARRIOR

White Wolf went on many raiding parties throughout his life with the Comanche. The last raid he went on was led by Buffalo Hump. Most of the bands came together for the big pow-wow. Buffalo Hump spoke to the gathered Comanche, "The Great Spirit has given me a vision of a great raid where we will deal the whites their final defeat. He has shown me that *The People* will drive the whites into the water." Four hundred Comanche warriors came together under the leadership of Buffalo Hump and swept across central Texas all the way to the Gulf Coast to the cities of Linville and Victoria, capturing many horses and killing many whites. They did drive some of the whites into the sea but it was not the complete victory that was in Buffalo Hump's vision.

When Buffalo Hump turned his warriors and the many captured horses back towards home, the Texas Rangers tried to cut them off from returning to Llano Estacado. The Rangers recovered just a fraction of the horses and killed only a few warriors. One Ranger erroneously reported there was close to 1,000 Indians in the raiding party. A wiser head skeptically observed that with that kind of force, the Comanche could have taken Austin and Houston.

There were many reports from ranchers, farmers and the Texas Rangers of a white man who rode with the Comanche. All the reports shared something in common. They spoke of a white Comanche who was a fearless rider and fighter. One Ranger was heard to say, "We would have killed a lot more of them red varmints if that white son of a bitch had not interfered."

The last band of Comanche who surrendered to the U.S. Army was led by Quanah and Red Elk. In 1875 they journeyed to Ft. Sill, Oklahoma where they made peace with Colonel R.S. McKenzie. McKenzie was a stocky bull of a man with a neatly trimmed, salt-and-pepper beard and mustache. After Col. McKenzie accepted their surrender he said, "You have a white man living among you. I want to talk to him."

Quanah and Red Elk relayed Col. McKenzie's request to White Wolf. White Wolf said, "I will not speak to him. I am only surrendering out of respect to you, Quanah, and to you, Red Elk."

Quanah said, "You must change your thinking, brother. The old way is no more. We must learn to live in the white man's world."

Red Elk nodded his head in agreement, "Quanah speaks wise words. You must follow them, my son."

When White Wolf prepared to meet with McKenzie, Ten Bears approached him carrying the Jackson family Bible. Ten Bears said, "Take the sacred book with you to see the white chief. It has great medicine. It will protect you."

When White Wolf met with Col. McKenzie, the soldier had a Comanche with him, Swift Antelope, who had learned the basics of the white man's language, to translate between the two men. White Wolf had never met Swift Antelope but he had heard the name before. He had heard that Swift Antelope was a man of honor. Swift Antelope had straight, black hair; coal black eyes and a very dark complexion. He was a very intimidating man.

Col. McKenzie said to White Wolf, translated by Swift Antelope, "You are a white man. You should leave the reservation and live in the white man's world. You need to learn to speak the white man's tongue. You could set a great example to the Comanche on living in their new world. I know you participated in raids against whites, but that will be forgiven if you choose to help the Comanche to find the path to lasting peace."

While White Wolf had his doubts about wanting to live in the white man's world. He said to Col. McKenzie, "I too want to speak the white man's tongue. Who will teach me? Swift Antelope?"

McKenzie replied, "No, he is just learning himself. Mrs. Forbes, the wife of one of my staff officers, Capt. Forbes, has volunteered to teach you English."

When White Wolf returned to the tribe, he met with Quanah and Red Elk in Quanah's tipi. As they shared the pipe, White Wolf said, "I spoke with McKenzie. One of the white women will teach me their language. He also said that I should leave *The People* and live in the white world. I will never do this. I will never leave my people!"

After a moment of thoughtful silence, Quanah spoke. "White Wolf, you are my most trusted friend and brother. For the good of *The People*, you must leave us and learn the white man's ways. This is the best service that you can do for *The People*."

Red Elk said, "My son, I say this with great sadness. You must leave us. I believe Quanah is right. I agree that you can help *The People* best by learning and teaching us the white man's way."

WHITE MAN'S WORLD

Quanah made an amazing transformation from basically living in the Stone Age to becoming a wealthy, respected and powerful man in the white man's world. Some of this could be attributed to the counsel of White Wolf. White Wolf introduced Quanah to Burk Burnett, a successful white rancher who established the Four Sixes Ranch. The Four Sixes became one of the largest cattle ranches in the southwest. Quanah and Burnett became friends. Quanah leased Indian land to Burnett to graze his cattle. This business arrangement caused both to prosper.

A great sadness in Quanah's life was when his mother, Cynthia Ann, was forcibly returned to her white family against her will. This was before Quanah became a powerful and influential man. She had lived for 24 years with the Comanche. She never adjusted to her new life back in white society. She longed to return to her Comanche family. She ultimately lost her will to live, starving herself to death.

Mrs. Forbes was tall and thin. She was not frightened in the least by the close personal contact that was required to teach the Comanche to read. Mrs. Forbes was amazed at how quickly White Wolf learned English. She had dedicated herself to teaching English to the Indians but she had never had a pupil who learned as fast as White Wolf. When she began teaching him to read by using her Bible as a text book, he showed her his own Bible.

After examining it, Mrs. Forbes said to him, "Where did you get this?"

White Wolf told her, "It belonged to my white father and mother."

Mrs. Forbes replied, "Do you know who they were or anything about them?"

White Wolf said, "No, they died when I was a baby." He did not tell her that they were killed by his Comanche family. He knew the white woman would not understand the Comanche way.

Mrs. Forbes excitedly said, "White Wolf, this book tells the names of you father and mother! They were Henry and Martha Jackson. They had named you Jacob. I bet they called you Jake. Your real name is Jake Jackson."

White Wolf corrected her, "No, my real name is White Wolf."

The next day, Col. McKenzie called White Wolf into his office. "Mrs. Forbes tells me that she has discovered your real name."

White Wolf stubbornly said, "My real name is White Wolf."

McKenzie replied, "White Wolf, I remember you telling me that Quanah and Red Elk wanted you to learn the ways of the white world so that you could help the Comanche learn to live in the white world. It would further that aim if you had a white man's name. Remember, you are white."

White Wolf considered what McKenzie said. Finally he responded, "I understand what you are saying, but I won't give up my Comanche name. I will continue to be known as White Wolf to the Comanche, but I will go by Jake Jackson to the whites."

THE FOUR
SIXES

W hen Burk Burnett heard about the white
Comanche who wanted to live in the white man's
world, he visited Jake at Ft Sill. Burnett was of
average height but muscular due to the physical nature of
years of living on the open range. His bushy white moustache
gave his face character. After the introductions, Burnett said
to Jake, "It is my understanding that you want to live in the
white man's world to help the Comanche learn to adjust to
their new life."

Jake nodded his head. "Yes, I believe that the Great Spirit
has given me this to do."

Burnett replied, "I'd like to help you and I'd like to help the
Comanche. I think you and yore people got a raw deal and I'd
like to do my part to square it. I am offering you a job at my
ranch. You interested?"

Jake liked the looks of Burk Burnett and replied without
hesitation, "I will come with you."

Burk outfitted Jake with clothing, horse and saddle. Burk
and Jake returned to the ranch's headquarters outside of

Wichita Falls in north Texas. Burk left Jake in the main house while he went to speak to his men in the sprawling bunk house. After explaining who Jake was, Burk said, "This man is comin' to work here. If anyone has a problem with that, draw your pay and clear out." Out of nineteen men, three started packing their gear. Burk turned to his ranch foreman, Isaac Harris and said, "Isaac, get these men paid and gone. Then get our new man squared away and show him the ropes."

Isaac commanded respect from the men but not from his ordinary appearance. There weren't any problems with cattle, horses or ranching that Isaac had not seen before. Men respected his knowledge and knew Isaac would know exactly what to do in any situation.

None of the remaining men had much to say to Jake but most were curious about this white Comanche. Isaac was pleasantly surprised at Jake's intelligence and his willingness to work the cattle. Jake only had to be shown something once to learn it. Jake became one of Isaac's most reliable and dependable hands.

The only thing that Isaac was a little hesitant about was giving Jake a gun. He knew that the men would be uneasy living with an armed Comanche. When enough time had passed that Isaac was comfortable with giving Jake a gun, he said to Jake as he handed Jake a Colt, holster and gun belt, "Do you know how to use one of these?"

Jake responded, "No, but I will learn."

Isaac set up three bottles on a ridge behind the bunk house. After showing Jake the basics, Isaac said, "See iffen you can hit one of them bottles."

Jake missed on his first shot but broke all three bottles with his next three shots. Isaac exclaimed, "Damn boy, are you sure you ain't never shot before?"

Jake replied, "No, this is my first time."

Isaac said with a grin, "Hell, you might oughta be givin' me lessons!" Isaac set up more bottles, then showed Jake the best way to draw his gun from the holster and fire. Again, Isaac was amazed at how fast Jake learned. After half a dozen repetitions, Jake was drawing his pistol and accurately firing in one smooth motion. Later Isaac told Burk, "I ain't never seen nobody take to shootin' like this kid. He is sumthin' special."

Whenever Jake had a few minutes, he practiced his draw. His draw became quicker than a lightening strike. The other men would occasionally see Jake practice his draw. They were amazed as his hand was now just a blur as he drew his gun.

The Four Sixes began losing cows to rustlers. Finally Burk told Isaac, "Take a couple of your best men and see if you can find the owlhoots that are stealing our beeves." Isaac chose Jake and Jim Ed Robinson.

Jim Ed's face was lined with wrinkles from a lifetime of exposure to the sun, but he had a kind look in his eyes that made people feel that they could trust him. Jim Ed and Isaac had worked together on other ranches before they signed on at the Four Sixes. Isaac knew that Jim Ed was steady and wouldn't get rattled in a pinch. He chose Jake based on gut instinct. He had never seen Jake get excited in any circumstances and he knew Jake was the best gun hand that he had.

The men rode to the last place that they knew where cattle had been stolen. They followed the trail of the outlaws for over twenty miles. The tracks lead into a box canyon that was lined by mesquite trees. Their sharp thorns made a natural barrier. A voice rang out from the cover of the mesquites, "Hold it right there boys and raise them hands!"

Isaac, Jim Ed and Jake cautiously lifted their hands. Six outlaws rode out of the brush and made a semi-circle around the captured men. One of the outlaws, Skeeter Burt, said, "Now git down from them cayuses and drop them guns real slow. And it better be slow enough that I can count the hairs on the back of yore hands."

Skeeter had a pock-marked face from a battle with small pox. Most women and some men couldn't look at his ugly face for long without averting their eyes.

Isaac and Jim Ed started to dismount but Jake's instincts told him that if they did, they would all be as good as dead. Instead Jake drew his pistol. Six shots blended together as one sound. All six outlaws had holes dead center of their chests. Skeeter clutched at his chest and hollered, "Dammit, I've been kilt!" It was hard to say who was the most shocked: the six outlaws who were starting to fall from their saddles or Isaac and Jim Ed.

Isaac whistled through his teeth and was the first to speak. "Boy, how in the hell did you do that?"

Jim Ed then said, "Jake, I ain't never seen or even heared of that kind of shootin'!" They looked at Jake and were further surprised as Jake looked like nothing had happened greater than slapping a mosquito. The men gathered up the stolen cattle and rode back to the ranch in silence. Isaac and Jim Ed were still in shock. Jake was not known for saying much anyway.

After Isaac and Jim Ed told Burk and the rest of the men what had happened, the story spread like wildfire. Soon it seemed the whole countryside had heard of the white Comanche gun hand that was working for Burk Burnett.

The cowhands for the Four Sixes began to trust and respect Jake, not for just his ability with a gun but for his work ethic. No man on the ranch could outwork Jake. The men began to genuinely like Jake. They began inviting him into town to visit the Yellow Dog Saloon. At first Jake didn't care much for the taste of whiskey but learned to appreciate its warm effects as long as he didn't drink too much or too fast.

One night Jake and some of the hands from the ranch were at the Yellow Dog drinking whiskey. They were seated at one big table when Ox Ploeger banged open the swinging doors and stomped into the saloon. Ox was a giant Swede who had blond hair and a handlebar mustache. His hair was so blond it was almost white. Ox was the acknowledged brawling champion of Wichita Falls. He had never been beaten. It was said that Ox, who was a blacksmith, could lift an anvil with one hand. When he fought, most of the time he would let his opponent hit him as often as they liked without defending himself. Ox would laugh uproariously during the assault, laughing harder with each blow. The fight would usually end with one punch from Ox. Whatever body part that Ox hit would break.

Ox put his hands on his hips and shouted, "I heared that there was some kinda bad-ass Injun in here! Stand up and fight if you ain't skeered!"

Jake started to get up but Jim Ed put a restraining hand on Jake's arm as he whispered, "Easy son, this is a stacked deck. Just let this blowhard have his say and he'll be on his way."

Ox continued when no one got to his feet, "I always knowed most Injuns were chickenshits. I guess what I heared 'bout this so-called bad-ass was a pack of lies. He's just like the rest of them redskins. They shoulda been called yellerskins!" Ox laughed uproariously at his own joke and looked around the room to see if he could figure out who the Indian was.

Jake threw off Jim Ed's hand as he rose to his feet. "I'm Jake Jackson if you're looking for me."

Ox looked him up and down, "Well hell, you're just a kid! You can't be what everybody is goin' on about! I don't know if it would even be worth my time to whip yore scrawny ass!" The look of unconcern on Jake's face finally got to Ox, "Boy, do you know who I am?"

Jake answered, "I don't know who you are but I know what you are."

Ox shouted, "And just what in the hell do you mean by that?" Jake moved away from the table so he would have room to move. "I figure your momma named you Ox because she knew you were going to be as dumb as an ox." The boys from the Four Sixes guffawed.

Ox charged in a fit of rage with his eyes bulging and his face purple. Unfortunately for Ox, Jake had seen this before, only it was from a bull buffalo out on the Llano Estacado. Jake used the same move to dodge Ox that he used on the buffalo and jumped on Ox's back as he drew his scalping knife from the sheaf in the small of his own back. Jake had Ox in a headlock with one arm as he pressed the edge of his blade to Ox's throat with his other hand. The sharp edge began to draw blood and Ox could feel its bite as blood started to trickle down his neck.

In a calm voice, Jake spoke. "The way I see it, Mr. Ox, you have two choices. One, I will cut your throat from ear to ear and then out of respect for my Comanche family, I will slice your scalp off and nail it to this saloon's wall. Your second choice is for us to smoke the peace pipe and I will buy you a drink."

Ox wasn't the quickest of thinkers but after he realized his predicament, he started to laugh. "Well hell, kid. That ain't much of a choice atall. Gimme that drink."

Jake slowly slid off his broad back wary of Ox continuing the fight but Ox stuck out one of his huge mitts and said, "Kid, you're all right in my book. You and me are gonna be friends."

BLACK JACK

J ake's fight with Ox further added to his growing reputation. He was gaining in respect from the white world, but there was also a less desirable result. Jake had now become a target for those who wanted to make their own reputation by killing him.

Black Jack Davis came from a family of outlaws. His father, Blackie Davis was hung by a posse when they found the old man herding stolen horses. His mother, Betty Davis, was one of the few women ever sentenced to prison in those days. She was caught with Blackie with the stolen horses. Betty barely escaped the hangman's noose that day. The posse debated on stringing her up too but decided to take her back into Jacksboro for trial. Betty was tried and sentenced to 20 years in prison, but she hung herself after serving less than a year.

Black Jack had two brothers and a sister. His brothers were thieves and murderers, and his sister was a whore who ended up dying of syphilis. Both of his brothers were hung, one legally after a trial and the other by vigilantes who didn't see the need for a trial.

Black Jack tracked down all the members of the posse that hung his father and sent his mother to jail, and killed them all in an ambush. Black Jack liked to brag, "The Davises always pay their debts."

Black Jack was not a big man, but his long black, curly hair made an impression. Most folks remembered him once they first saw him. Black Jack began his career as a gunslinger, shooting down some local toughs who fancied themselves as fast with a gun. Black Jack discovered he was a good hand with a gun and he actually was a fast draw.

As was the wont of the Davis clan, Black Jack wanted to get rich quick. The fact that this attitude had resulted in the deaths of his entire family was lost on Black Jack. Black Jack just figured they were unlucky.

Black Jack thought to himself, "I need to outdraw and kill somebody famous. That would git me everything that should already be mine. I keep gittin' cheated outta what's mine. Everybody's braggin' on this Injun like he's somethin' special. Iffen I kill that son of a bitch, folks will sit up and know who I am."

Jake and the boys were in the Yellow Dog one Saturday night when Black Jack pushed through the swinging doors and walked over to where Jake was sitting. "Injun, git off yore ass. I'm gonna send you to the happy huntin' ground."

Jake responded, "Mister, I don't know you. What do you think I've done to you?"

Black Jack crouched as he bellowed, "Quit yore damn stallin' and git up or I'll plug you right where you sit!"

Jake studied Black Jack as he slowly rose to his feet. The rest of the men scrambled out of the line of fire except for

Isaac and Jim Ed. They were seated on each side of Jake but were not concerned about stray bullets. The smiles on their faces showed neither of them thought that this fool would even get off a shot.

Jake said to Black Jack, "Mister, you're making a bad mistake. It's not too late for you to turn around and forget this stupid idea of yours. If I have to shoot, I will not try to wound you. I will shoot to kill you."

Black Jack laughed and said, "I ain't worried about that none!" When he finished, Black Jack went for his gun. He barely got his hand on the grip of his pistol when a shot rang out. The only way that anyone knew that two shots had been fired were the hole in his chest and half of his throat was also torn away. Black Jack was dead on his feet.

As he fell backwards from the force of the bullets, it marked the passing of the last member of the sorry Davis family. The best thing about all of them being dead was they were officially out of the gene pool.

MACY
KATHLEEN

O ne afternoon while in town picking up supplies for
the ranch, Jake saw a beautiful black-haired woman
coming down the wooden sidewalk twirling a pink
parasol. He later found out her name was Macy Kathleen
Bishop. Macy Kathleen was one of the local school teachers.
Macy Kathleen, dressed in lace, was the perfect picture of a
lady. In addition to her china-doll face, her long, black hair
was her most striking characteristic. She had never cut her
hair except to even it up. When she let it down, her hair fell
all the way to her ankles.

When Jake lived as a Comanche, he had numerous sexual
encounters with various Comanche girls. Some would sneak
into his tipi late at night or give him a look to follow them
as they headed into the woods. None of them interested Jake
enough for him to pursue taking them as a wife. Jake was
known in the village as being hard to please when it came
to women, much to the chagrin of all the young women of
the tribe.

When he and Jim Ed were about to meet Macy Kathleen on the sidewalk, Jake tipped his hat and politely said, "Ma'am." She blushed and ducked her head as she hurried past Jake. Jake turned and watched her walk away. He was captivated by her in a way that no other female had ever affected him. He asked Jim Ed, "Do you know who that woman is?"

Jim Ed replied, "Shore, she's old Billy Bishop's daughter, Macy Kathleen. Bishop's got a spread up around the Red River. It's a small outfit. He only runs about five hundred head. Burk and old Billy are long-time friends."

When they got back to the ranch, Jake went to the big house to talk to Burk. "Burk, I saw this woman in town. Jim Ed said her name was Macy Kathleen Bishop and that you and her pa were good friends. I would like to meet her. Can you arrange that?"

Burk scratched his head and said, "If I vouch for you, I'm sure Billy will let you call on his daughter."

The next day was a bright and sunny. Burk told Jake, "Saddle up, son. We're gonna call on Billy Bishop."

When the two men arrived at the small ranch house, they dismounted and tied their horses to the hitching rail. Billy heard them ride up and came out the front door adjusting his suspenders, "Well howdy, Burk, you ol polecat! Long time no see! What brings you up to these parts? Billy was portly and bald and his look was welcoming.

Burk strode over to Billy and they shook hands and clapped each other on the back. Burk said, "Well, I've actually come on sorta family matter. This here boy is one of my best hands.

His name is Jake Jackson. Jake seen Macy Kathleen in town and he wants your permission to call on her."

Jake stuck out his hand and as Billy shook it, Billy's forehead furrowed as he studied Jake.

Jake said, "Nice to meet you, sir."

Billy replied with a frown, "Now, ain't you the boy who everyone's talkin' about shooting people or whippin' their ass?"

Burk broke in, "Now Billy, them boys who Jake shot was rustlers, and if Jake hadn't shot 'em, they'd a killed not only him but Isaac and Jim Ed too. Isaac and Jim Ed will tell you he saved their hides. Jake did what he had to do. As far as I'm concerned, he's a damn hero. And do you know whose ass he whipped? It was that jug-headed Ox Ploeger. Jake beat him without throwin' a punch! Can you imagine that?"

Billy slowly stroked his jaw in thought. "Well, I jest don't know. I knowed he would have to be a good man or you wouldn't have brung him up here to meet me. You speakin' for him means a bunch. The onlyest thing is, the boy sure seems to attract trouble. A man don't want trouble for his daughter. He wants her to be happy."

Jake finally spoke after a few minutes of silence. "Mr. Bishop, I can understand where you're coming from. If you will allow me to court your daughter, I will treat her with respect. At any time if you or she wants me to stop seeing her, I will stop."

Billy looked back at Burk. Burk was nodding his head yes and grinning. Billy grinned a little and said, "Okay, son. Since you come so highly recommended, we will give it a try. Mary

Kathleen will be comin' home this weekend for a visit. If it's alright with her, I will send word to you and you can call on her at the Candlelight Inn. That's the boarding house in town where she's stayin'."

The Candlelight Inn was owned and operated by the Widow Brown. The Widow had a pinched, sour face that always had a perpetual frown on it. Some folks speculated that if she ever smiled it would have caused her face to crack. No one was sure what her first name was and she never volunteered it. She was respectfully called Mrs. Brown by everyone. No one knew anything about her past except they knew her husband had passed away. She was already a widow when she moved to Wichita Falls over twenty years ago.

Mrs. Brown didn't put up with any shenanigans at her establishment. Any boarder that showed bad behavior, such as being drunk, would be thrown out on his or her ear. She also had several young ladies like Macy Kathleen living there. Mrs. Brown was like a mother hen protecting her chicks when it came to her young ladies.

After handshakes all around, they all had a cup of coffee. Burk and Billy laughed as they reminisced about old times. On the ride back to the ranch, Jake said, "The Comanche way is much better. If an Indian brings enough horses to a girl's father, the father just gives the girl to you!"

Burk laughed long and hard about that and allowed it would make things easier.

That weekend Macy Kathleen rented a buckboard from the livery stable and made the hour drive to see her father. Most women were afraid of making that kind of trip by themselves, but Macy Kathleen never gave it a second thought. She carried a pistol and a rifle and she knew how to use them. Billy had seen to that when she was growing up on the ranch. Macy Kathleen had plugged many snakes, bobcats and coyotes. Once, she even killed a mountain lion that was sizing her up for its supper. Handling guns was as natural to her as the sun coming up every morning.

After they traded hugs and she settled down in her favorite chair with a cup of tea, Billy said, "I had me some visitors this week, old Burk Burnett and a young fella who works for him. Seems like this young fella wants my permission to call on you. I told 'em that it was alright by me, seein' as how Burk was vouching for him, but I'd have to talk to you to see iffen you was interested."

Macy Kathleen started to correct her father's English because that was what she was used to doing as a school teacher, but thought better of it as she knew it was a lost cause. "What's his name, Pa?"

Billy replied, "The boy's name is Jake Jackson." Macy Kathleen froze for just the tiniest of moments. She knew who Jake was. She had seen him a number of times in town. Her pulse always quickened when she looked at him because she thought Jake was the most handsome and exciting man she'd ever seen. Those were her exact thoughts when she met Jake on the sidewalk that day. When Jake spoke and tipped his hat, she blushed and hurried by because she was petrified that he would know what she was thinking. Finally Macy Kathleen said to Billy, "Let me think about it. I'll say yes or no before I leave to go back into town." Actually, she already knew she was going to say yes.

Sunday afternoon, as Macy Kathleen was getting ready to go back into town, she said to Billy, "Pa, you can tell Mr. Jackson he may call on me at the boarding house."

The next day, Billy was surprised to see Jake ride up. When Jake got down off his horse, Billy laughingly said, "Well hell boy, I reckon I know why you're here. You don't waste no time do you?"

As Jake shook Billy's hand, Jake said, "No sir, I don't. If something needs to be done, I like to get it done."

Billy replied, "Macy Kathleen said she would see you. You can call on her at the boarding house. But boy—and you best hear me good on this—nothing better happen to my little girl! I wouldn't take too kindly to that."

Jake responded, "Mr. Bishop, I can assure you I will protect your daughter with my life. Nothing will happen to her as long as I'm alive."

Billy studied Jake's face and said, "Jake, I believe what you're sayin'. I just have a feelin' I can trust you."

What neither Billy nor Macy Kathleen knew was that Jake had been watching from the brush when Macy Kathleen left the ranch to go back to town the day before. He kept out of sight but he wanted to make sure she got home safe. Jake rode back to the Four Sixes after seeing her enter the boarding house.

MEETING
AT THE
CANDLELIGHT

T he next night, Jake knocked at the front door of the Candlelight Inn. Mrs. Brown opened the door and said, "How can I help you, young man?" Mrs. Brown knew who Jake was as she had already been told by Macy Kathleen to expect Jake to come calling.

Jake took his hat off and replied, "Ma'am, I'm Jake Jackson. I came to see Macy Kathleen Bishop. She said it was alright for me to call on her."

Mrs. Brown gave Jake a stern look and said, "Mr. Jackson, please come have a seat in the parlor, but before I go see if Macy Kathleen can see you, you need to know the rules of the house. I will not put up with any disrespectful behavior. When you come here to see her, I will be watching you. Do you understand me?"

Jake managed to weakly croak out, "Yes, ma'am."

As Jake settled into one of the big upholstered chairs, he thought to himself, *Mrs. Brown might be a match for Kicking*

Squaw. In about fifteen minutes, Macy Kathleen walked into the room and greeted Jake, "Mr. Jackson."

Jake had already faced death many times in his young life and he was afraid of no man, but he suddenly found himself weak in the knees as he stood and extended his hand, "Miss Bishop, it's nice to meet you."

Macy Kathleen had been entranced staring at Jake's eyes when she realized that they had been shaking hands too long and she abruptly pulled her hand away. As they both sat down, Jake finally broke the awkward silence when he said, "Miss Bishop, would it be alright if I called you Macy Kathleen?"

Despite hearing Mrs. Brown harrumphing from the next room, Macy Kathleen answered, "That would be fine, Mr. Jackson." Jake quickly replied, "Please call me Jake."

Over the next two months, Jake would call on Macy Kathleen every Friday night at the Candlelight Inn under the supervision of Mrs. Brown. Despite an inordinate amount of harrumphing from the other room, Jake and Macy Kathleen got to know each other. Each was hungry for information about the other.

Macy Kathleen began inviting Jake out to her father's ranch on the weekends, away from the prying eyes and ears of the Widow Brown. Billy gradually began letting the young couple have more and more time alone. He even looked the other way at the times when he caught them kissing. The more Billy was around Jake, the better he liked him.

After six months of proper courting, Jake rode out to see Billy on a Friday morning. Jake said, "Billy, I'm in love with

Macy Kathleen. I would like to have your permission to ask her to marry me."

Billy had known this was coming eventually, as he could see how much his daughter loved Jake, but he didn't know it would be this soon. There was also a small knot in the pit of his stomach when he thought of the two of them getting married. It was fear, but Billy didn't know why he was afraid. Despite that feeling of dread, Billy grinned and said as he shook Jake's hand, "Of course son, welcome to the family."

That evening Jake went on his usual visit with Macy Kathleen at the boarding house. During the visit, she thought there was something odd about the look in Jake's eyes. Finally she said, "Okay Jake Jackson, something is going on. What are you up to?"

Jake just shrugged his shoulders and grinned, "I don't know what you're talking about. Can't a man have a look on his face without some woman thinking that he's up to something?"

Macy Kathleen narrowed her eyes and replied, "Yes, a man certainly can, but I'm not suspicious of most men. Just you!"

Jake again responded with a shrug and an even wider grin.

The next morning, Jake showed up at the Candlelight Inn to escort Macy Kathleen to her father's ranch. He tied his horse to the back of the buckboard and climbed into the driver's seat. Mrs. Brown was peering out on of the upstairs windows when she saw Jake climb up next to Macy Kathleen. The Widow Brown harrumphed as loudly as she possibly could, but the young couple was out of earshot, although she startled several of her boarders who were sleeping late. They came busting out of their rooms with guns drawn wanting to know what that God-awful noise was.

They took advantage of the privacy of the drive to the ranch by caressing, hugging and kissing each other along the way. When they got to the ranch, Jake called her into what passed for a parlor. When Billy heard that, he slipped out the door and went to tend to some imagined business at the barn. Macy Kathleen's hand flew to cover her mouth as Jake went down on one knee. Jake held her other hand, looked up at her and said, "Macy Kathleen Bishop, will you marry me?"

Despite the tears flowing down her face, Macy Kathleen managed to get out, "Yes, my darling, a thousand times yes!"

Jake jumped to his feet, and as they embraced, he whispered in her ear how much he loved her.

Macy Kathleen broke away from Jake and shouted, "Pa! Pa! Where are you Pa?"

Jake said, "I think Billy went to the barn." She ran to the barn to tell Billy the good news and a beaming Jake followed. Billy kissed and hugged her and almost took Jake's arm off shaking his hand. Jake gave Macy Kathleen the engagement ring that was her mother's. Billy had made a special request that Jake use that ring.

When Jake told Burk that he and Macy Kathleen were going to get married, Burk smiled and said, "I've been expectin' this, son. I had my eye on a thousand acre plot on my place that has good water and grass. I'm deedin' it over to you, along with five hundred head of cows and a couple of range bulls to help you get started as a rancher." Jake started to protest but Burk cut him off. "This ain't no gift. You can pay me back outta the money you make ranchin'. We'll worry 'bout the details later and I don't want to hear nothing else about it. Also, you're gonna need someone to help you there. I know you got some money saved up and can afford a hand. I would recommend Jim Ed. We got enough hands around here to make it without him and I think he would throw in with you iffen you asked him."

Jim Ed did take Jake up on his offer and the two of them begin the task of building a small ranch house, barn, bunk house and corral. After they had hauled in all the lumber they needed from Wichita Falls, they had just begun construction when they noticed a small dust cloud on the horizon, back in the direction of the Four Sixes headquarters. It turned out to be twenty of the ranch hands coming to help them with the building. With that much help, they built the houses, barn and corrals in two days.

The wedding saw a huge turnout of people including Quanah, Red Elk, Prairie Flower, Ten Bears and Kicking Squaw. Burk and most of the Four Sixes cowboys were there. The most surprising thing about the wedding was the Widow Brown attended and cried through the whole ceremony.

After the wedding, Jake and Macy Kathleen settled in to ranch life. She had resigned her position as a school teacher to become a full-time wife and future mother. Jim Ed slept in the bunk house, although he took all his meals with Jake and Macy Kathleen at the main house.

Macy Kathleen turned out to be an excellent cook. Every once in a while this created a small problem with Jake and Jim Ed jostling each other to be first in line to eat, especially when she had baked an apple pie. Sometimes Mary Kathleen would have to reprimand them. "Boys! Boys! Stop that pushing! For the life of me, I don't know why y'all act this way. Has either one of you ever left my table hungry?"

BLOODY BILL

One day Jake had ridden into town by himself to pick up some supplies. As he walked down the street, he heard what sounded like muffled screams down an alley and behind the dry goods store. When Jake walked around behind the store, he saw three men groping a young woman. Their hands were all over her body and one of the men had his hand clamped against her mouth as she tried to scream. Jake pulled one of his Peacemakers and the men came to attention when they heard the pistol cock. In a calm voice Jake said, "You three polecats turn her loose before I shoot your hands off her."

The three men were Bloody Bill Clark, Frog Evans and Peg-leg Elliott. Frog, who came by his name honestly as his face resembled a frog—complete with a green tint—said, "Mister, iffen you know what's good fer ya, you'd best mind yore own damn business."

Peg-leg joined in, "Yeah, you don't know who you're messin with." Peg-leg had lost his leg below the knee during a drunken stupor when he fell under a freight wagon. The wheel of the big wagon severed the bottom of his leg. Peg-leg whittled a peg so that he could get around until he saw a man with a store-bought one. Peg-leg killed him for it.

Before Jake could answer, Bloody Bill interrupted, "Now hold on boys, this here is Jake Jackson. Mr. Jackson, we were jest funning the gal. We don't mean no harm."

Bloody Bill had run with thieves and killers most of his life. It took somebody special to distinguish himself in that crowd. His pards gave him his nickname because his answer to everything was murder. Bloody Bill had killed men, women and children. Frog and Peg-leg realized their lives were in danger as Jake Jackson was nobody to trifle with, and they immediately let the girl go.

The girl ran to Jake and hid behind him. The three men started to walk away. Jake stopped them by saying, "Stop right there. I didn't say you could go."

Bloody Bill turned and warily asked, "What do you want?"

Jake said, "You roughed this gal up and what I want is an apology to her by each of you."

Frog snorted, "The hell I will. I ain't apologizing to nobody."

Jake's pistol barked as he shot off Frog's left ear. Frog was dancing around holding what was left of his ear and screaming bloody murder. Jake spoke again, "I'm just going to give you a couple of chances for a nice sincere apology. If you don't, I will shoot you three times. The first shot will take off one of your ears. The second shot will take off the other ear. The third shot will between your eyes."

Frog screamed at Jake, "You son of a bitch, you shot me!" A second shot rang out and Frog's other ear joined his first one in the dirt at his feet. Frog put up his hands and said, "Okay! Okay! I'm sorry!"

Jake responded, "Don't tell me. You didn't rough me up. Tell her."

Frog said to the girl who was peeking out from behind Jake, "Sorry Miss."

Peg-leg was next. "Sorry, ma'am, we wuz just funning."

Bloody Bill said, "Truly sorry, we shouldn'tna done that."

Jake then nodded his head that they could go. After they got out of earshot, Frog said to Bloody Bill, "I can remember a day when you'da killed a man for talkin' to you that way."

Bloody Bill replied, "Who said I ain't gonna kill him? But not today, 'cause the odds are agin us, but there will come a day when I'm gonna even up the score."

What burned the three thugs even more was that there happened to be several witnesses to the whole incident. The report of what happened swept the town. They were now a laughingstock, although all laughed behind their backs and not to their faces.

Married life could not have gone any better. The marriage bed sometimes caused Jake to begin work for the day a little late. Jake just could not get enough of Macy Kathleen and she could not get enough of him. Jim Ed would pretend not to notice but Jake knew he could figure it out.

Nine months to the day of their marriage, Macy Kathleen gave birth to a fine baby boy with blond hair and gray eyes. Unbeknownst to the happy couple, Macy Kathleen said the exact same thing to Jake as his mother said to his father when Jake was born, "Jake, he's you made over."

Jake named his new son Hunter. Jake loved to play with the baby and dreamed about all the things they would do together as Hunter grew older. Most babies are more attached to their mothers than anybody else. Hunter loved his mother but had an especially big smile whenever he grabbed one of Jake's fingers. Jake had the first ten years of Hunter's life planned out. Not only did he want Hunter to be as good as he was in hunting, riding and shooting, Jake wanted him to be better.

Bloody Bill Clark, Frog Evans and Peg-leg Elliott silently sat on their horses on a far ridge studying the layout of Jake's ranch. Frog said, "I sure would like me some of that squaw of hisn. I bet she's some fine piece of ass."

Peg-leg replied, "She ain't no squaw, dumbass. She's a white woman and Jackson is a white man."

Bloody Bill added, "You jest do as I say and you'll git all of her you want."

Jim Ed had ridden to the farthest part of the ranch looking for strays. He did not know that hidden in the tree line were three assassins. Bloody Bill lined him up in the sights of his Winchester rifle. Jim Ed heard the gunshot but nothing else as the world around him turned to black and death claimed him. Jim Ed's body slowly slipped from his horse.

Bloody Bill, Frog and Peg-leg rode up and dismounted to inspect the body. Bloody Bill fired a slug from his pistol into Jim Ed's head just to make sure he was dead. Frog took Jim Ed's kerchief and wiped Jim Ed's blood all over his saddle.

Peg-leg then fired his gun directly behind Jim Ed's horse and the horse took off at a gallop headed back to the ranch house. As the three men remounted and headed back into hiding, Bloody Bill said, "Now we git to see iffen Mr. Jake Jackson is such a big man after all."

Jake was working on the corral when Jim Ed's horse galloped up. Jake grabbed the reins and saw all the blood on the saddle. He turned the horse into the corral and ran into the house. "Macy Kathleen, something has happened to Jim Ed! His horse just showed up and there's blood all over the saddle. I've got to go find him."

Macy Kathleen urged him, "Hurry Jake, go get him. Dear God, please let Jim Ed be all right!" As she watched Jake strap on his guns and run back outside, she had a bad feeling in the pit of her stomach.

Jim Ed's horse was spent, so Jake had to saddle a fresh horse. He leaped into the saddle and galloped off in the direction that Jim Ed's horse had come from. Jake had to slow up slightly to back trail the horse. He was looking ahead when he spotted something that didn't look like it belonged. As he got closer, he saw it was Jim Ed's body. As he jumped down from his horse to see if his friend was still alive, three rifle shots rang out and three bullets thumped into his body. Somehow Jake managed to stand back up. When he did, three more shots were fired with all three slugs finding their marks. Jake crumpled to the ground.

Bloody Bill laughed and said to his grinning companions, "Well, I guess that son of a bitch ain't as great as everybody thinks he is. Let's go make sure he's dead."

Frog responded, "Hell Bill, that's a waste of time. Nobody can take six slugs from a rifle and live. That bastard is dead. Besides, I can't wait to git me some of that fine woman of his."

Bloody Bill chuckled, "I guess yore right. Let's go tend to our business."

Mary Kathleen was standing on the porch watching for Jake when she saw the three men riding up. She didn't know them so she stepped back inside and got the rifle that was kept next to the door. She had the rifle pointing at the three men when they rode up to the house. "What do you boys want?"

Bloody Bill took his hat off and said respectfully, "Are you Mrs. Jackson?"

Macy Kathleen replied, "Yes, I'm Mrs. Jackson. What do you need?"

Bloody Bill continued, "Ma'am, we found Mr. Jackson and he's hurt bad. He wanted us to come fetch you."

Macy Kathleen gasped, "Would you men hook up our buckboard while I go get our baby?" She put down the gun as she rushed back in the house to get Hunter.

Instead of going out to the barn to hook up the buckboard, the men dismounted and silently followed her into the house. Macy Kathleen was preoccupied with Hunter and didn't notice the men until two hands grabbed her and turned her around.

She screamed, "What are you doing? We have to go help my husband!"

Bloody Bill laughed as he slapped her. "Yore damn husband is dead. We know 'cause we kilt him. But you'll be glad to know that before he died he told us to help ourselves to his nice young wife."

All the men laughed as they tore off her clothes and tied her naked and spread-eagled on the bed. Frog was the first one with his pants down. He climbed on top of Macy Kathleen, saying, "Now honey, yore in for a real treat. I spect you'll be thankin' me when I'm done." He had to grab her hair to pull her mouth away as she was screaming and trying to bite him. I

t was a long afternoon for Macy Kathleen. She was sure Jake would rescue her but when he didn't show up, she knew he had to be dead. The men used her repeatedly in ways natural and unnatural.

Finally, Bloody Bill said, "Alright boys we done had our fun. Now it's time to clear out before somebody comes callin' on these good folks."

Peg-leg said, "What do we do with the bitch?"

Bloody Bill replied, "She's seen us. What do you think we're gonna do? We don't want her tellin' who done this." He walked over to her, pulled his knife and cut Macy Kathleen's throat.

As her blood reddened the bed, Blood Bill went over to the baby and stabbed him until he was dead. Peg-leg said,

"Why'd you go and do that fer? That kid couldn'tna told nobody nothin."

Bloody Bill responded, "Mr. Jake Jackson shoulda thought about that fore he messed with Bloody Bill Clark."

Isaac and two of the hands saw the buzzards circling and decided to ride over to see what was dead. He needed to know if it was one of their cows. Isaac was horrified to see that it was Jake and Jim Ed, all shot to pieces. Isaac jumped down from his horse, exclaiming, "Dear God! Dear God! Dear God!"

After looking Jake and Jim Ed over, he could see that Jim Ed was dead but he saw a slight rising and falling of Jake's chest. Isaac ordered one of the men, "Tom, ride into town and bring the doc straight out here. Jake is still alive, but I don't know how long he's got left. Tell the doc to hurry and you see that he does." To the other man, he said, "Bob, you ride back to the ranch and tell Burk what has happened. Tell him to bring the buckboard and some men."

Isaac pulled his shirt off and started to cut it into bandages. He tended Jake's wounds as best he could, trying to stop the bleeding.

In an hour, old Doc Murphy pulled up in his buckboard followed by Tom. As he started to examine Jake, Isaac worriedly asked, "Can he make it, doc?"

Doc Murphy replied, "Hell, I don't see how he's made it this long." In a few minutes, Doc said, "The boy has six bullets in him. His only chance is if those slugs are taken out now and I don't know if that will even help. Plus, me cutting them out may kill him anyway. But we have no choice. They've got to come out and they've got to come out now." Doc paused and then continued, "You boys build me a fire so I can sterilize my instruments. I've got to operate on him now."

As Doc started cutting out the bullets with Tom doing whatever the Doc needed him to do to help, Burk rode up with ten of his men. Burk said to Isaac, "Bob is a little ways behind us with the buckboard. How is Jake doing?"

Isaac shook his head, "It ain't good, Burk."

Burk asked, "Isaac, have you got any ideas how this happened?"

Isaac replied, "I looked around a little. The best I can tell, it was three men. I found some empty cartridges over in them trees. I think the three men dry-gulched the boys from there. There's one other thing, Burk and it's bad….real bad."

Burk said, "Well what the hell is it?"

Isaac grimly said, "The tracks of them three killers are headed toward Jake's house."

Burk swung back into his saddle saying, "You five boys stay here. The rest of you, come with me." Burk spurred his horse and lit out for Jake's ranch at a dead run. All six horses were in a lather as they pulled up to the ranch house. Burk tied up his horse at the hitching rail and told his men, "You boys get down and look around. I'm goin' in the house."

Burk saw that the front door was standing open. He knew that wasn't good. When he saw the bodies of Macy Kathleen and Hunter, he stepped back out on the porch with tears streaming down his face. Burk was a hardened veteran of the western frontier. He had seen many atrocities, but this affected him like no other. His men couldn't imagine something so awful that it would make him cry. Burk told his men, "Don't come in here until I tell you." Burk cut Macy Kathleen's restraints and cleaned the two bodies as best that he could. He then wrapped them in clean blankets.

Burk knew he had to ride out to tell Billy Bishop what had happened. He thought to himself that he would trade the Four Sixes if he didn't have to bring this sad news to old Billy. It turned out to be worse than he could have imagined.

THE
COMANCHE
WAY

When Burk rode up to Billy's house, Billy had a big grin for his old friend. When Billy saw the look on Burk's face, it felt like an icy hand started to squeeze his heart. Try as he might, Burk could not stop the tears as he said, "Old friend, I would rather be horse whipped than afta tell you this." Burk's voice caught and he had to pause.

Billy was terrified but said, "Spit it out. Is it Macy Kathleen?"

Burk finally found his voice. "Yes, it's her and the baby. They've both been killed."

There were no words to describe the impact of Macy Kathleen's and Hunter's deaths had on Billy. He was never the same after that. Macy Kathleen was the light of his life. Now, that light had been snuffed out. Later in life, when Billy passed away, Burk spoke at his old friend's funeral. "I wish I could tell you that Billy had just died but I'm afraid he died the day I had to tell him about Macy Kathleen."

Billy asked that his daughter and grandson be buried behind his ranch house. It seemed that half the countryside attended Macy Kathleen and Hunter's funeral, including all of Jake's Comanche family.

Jake clung to life by the narrowest of threads. He couldn't be moved, so they had to set up camp and tend to him right where he had been found. Doc stayed with Jake for three days, but finally told Burk, "I've done all I can do and I've got other patients who need me. Frankly, it's now up to Jake whether he lives or dies."

Jake stayed at the makeshift camp for two weeks, with Burk rotating his cowboys in shifts to look after him. When Burk thought he was strong enough to travel, they gently loaded Jake in a wagon and slowly drove him back to the Four Sixes. Jake had been in and out of consciousness for the two weeks. He would be awake long enough for them to feed him but he wasn't able to speak. Burk put Jake in the guest room at the main house.

One night, Burk heard his name being called. It was Jake. Jake looked up from his bed and haltingly said, "M... Ma... cy... Hun... ter." Burk just looked at Jake and shook his head. Burk couldn't speak but he could see by the look in Jake's eyes that he understood. Burk saw a look of fury and coldness come in Jake's eyes and on his face that was frightening to see.

One day Burk, Isaac and the boys came in from the range to find Jake sitting on the porch waiting for them. He should not have been up. Doc had said that it would take him a good six months to be up and around. It had only been six weeks. They were shocked at Jake's appearance. He was dressed only in a breechcloth and moccasins but that wasn't the shocking part. The shocking part was his face was painted black. Burk knew that black was the Comanche color of war. They all knew that Jake was raised as a Comanche but this was the first time they had seen hard evidence of his upbringing.

Jake spoke first. "Burk, I am giving you back my land and cattle. You also may have the houses, barn and corrals. I have no further need for them. I will no longer be a rancher." Burk responded, "Son, I think I know how you feel and what you got in mind, but you can't do it like this. Them boys have a six week head start on you. You have no idea where they've gone." Jake's face was like a stone. Burk continued, "At least let me send some of the boys with you. And where are your guns? You're gonna need your guns."

Jake replied, "My friend, I thank you for your offer. You have always been kind to me. But, I will have to turn you down. I will not be taking my guns, either. The work I must do will be up close. I do not want to kill these men at a distance. I want to look them in the eye when they die." Jake unhitched his horse and leaped on his back. The horse was wearing a rope bridle but no saddle. Jake was going to avenge Macy Kathleen and Hunter in the Comanche way.

Billy had come to the Four Sixes on several occasions to see Jake and how he was doing, but each time Jake had been asleep. Billy had not had a conversation with Jake since the murders. Billy was fixing a saddle in the barn. He didn't hear

Jake come up. He just looked up and Jake was standing there. At first Billy went for his gun because of the way Jake was dressed and his painted face, but suddenly Billy recognized Jake. Jake said, "Billy, I am full of shame. I promised to keep your daughter safe and I did not. I am sorry for what I have done to you."

Billy stood up and embraced Jake. "Son, you are not to blame. I know how much you loved Macy Kathleen and Hunter. Their deaths were not your fault." The look on Jake's face told Billy that he felt he did not take care of his wife and child and that he was responsible.

Jake asked, "Before I go, may I see their graves?"

Billy took him out behind the main house where Billy had built a small fenced private cemetery. It had two graves. While Jake looked at the graves in silence, Billy said, "Don't worry none about them. I come out here every day to talk to them. They're doing good." The two men looked at each other, sharing a sadness that could not be put into words. As Jake rode off, Billy called after him, "Take care of yourself, son!"

To most men, locating the three killers would seem like an impossible task with a trail that is six weeks old, but Jake was not like most men. While lying in bed waiting to get strong enough to walk, he had formulated a plan to extract his revenge. Jake knew that Bloody Bill, Frog and Peg-leg were the only ones that had a grudge against him. Jake now wished that he had killed them on the spot. He also knew that the scum in Ft. Worth usually came together in a dilapidated old bar by the apt name of The Outlaw Saloon.

Jake rode through the streets of Ft. Worth as a Comanche painted for war. People were gasping in astonishment as women hustled their children off the streets. Jake heard one man say, "God Almighty! I believe that there is Jake Jackson! Member, he was raised by Injuns. I heared his wife and boy was murdered. I'd hate to be the ones he's after."

Jake tied up his horse outside of The Outlaw and pushed through the swinging doors. The piano player was playing a lively tune of "Buffalo Gal" but stopped cold when he saw Jake. The rest of the people in the bar froze.

Jake recognized a table full of thieves and cutthroats. Before anyone could react, Jake was at the table and jerked up the first one he came to. He whirled him around and held him with one arm while his other hand pressed the edge of his scalping knife against the terrified man's throat. Jake spoke in a calm voice which had an unnerving effect. "Boys, this is how it's going to go. I am going to ask you the whereabouts of three men. If you give me the right answer, you live. If you give me the wrong answer, I will come back and kill you and you won't get another chance. If you don't answer at all, I will cut your throat and hang your scalp from my horse's mane. If I have to kill this man, I will go around the table cutting each of your throats until someone tells me what I want to know." Jake paused and then spoke again, "If you don't know me, my name is Jake Jackson. Some of you might think you can get to your gun before I can get to you. That would be a mistake on your part."

Jake paused again to gauge the eyes of the five men sitting at the table to see if someone was measuring him to see if they thought they could pull their gun in time. Jake could see all five of these men were too scared to try anything. In the meantime, the bar had emptied, with people running and diving out of any exit they could find.

Jake started to press his knife deeper in the man's throat and said, "Where is Bloody Bill Clark, Frog Evans and Peg-leg Elliott?"

The outlaw stammered out a lie, "I... don't... know." Jake slashed his throat and seemingly in one motion sliced off his scalp. He tossed the scalp on the table and jerked up the second man with blinding speed. The second man immediately started talking as he was peeing in his pants, "The last I heared, them three was rustlin' cows out in west Texas close to Pecos." Several of the other men seated at the table nodded their heads in agreement.

Jake pushed the second man back down in his chair. "I'll see if you boys are telling me the truth. If you're not, you can count on seeing me again. Oh, by the way, I would be real disappointed if you boys didn't tell the sheriff that I had to kill this man because he attacked me. I expect all of you to say it was self-defense. Are we clear on the story to the sheriff?" All the men vigorously nodded their heads in agreement.

When Sheriff Pat Waters questioned them, he asked, "Boys, what happened? I don't believe I've ever had nobody scalped in town before. What happened to Jesse?"

All five men started talking excitedly at the same time. The only thing that Pat kept hearing over and over was "self-defense."

Pat shouted them down as he said, "Are you boys saying that Jesse attacked Jake Jackson? With what? His gun is still in his holster! That don't make no sense."

Pat could see they were scared shitless and they all kept saying, "It was self-defense." Pat threw his hands up disgustedly as he walked out. The only thing that kept him from pursuing it further was that he knew Jesse needed killing and that left one less thug for him to deal with.

Jake rode back to the Four Sixes and spoke to Burk, "Burk, I've got to go to west Texas. I need six horses and some grub."

Burk replied, "Son, you can have anything you want."

Jake quickly rounded up the food and the horses and struck out for west Texas. Normally, Pecos was a week's hard ride. By switching off on the horses without dismounting, and only stopping long enough for a few hours' sleep, Jake made it in three days. Jake was fueled by a burning anger that penetrated the depth of his very being. He also made the entire trip without being seen by anybody. Jake wanted it to be a surprise when he showed up.

As Jake was scouting the countryside around Pecos, he spotted two cowboys using a straight iron on a half a dozen cows they had stolen. A straight iron was used to alter brands on cattle. Just having possession of a straight iron would get a man hung in some parts of Texas. These two rustlers had shot and killed two innocent cowboys from ambush to steal the cattle.

Jake waited until after dark. The two rustlers were wrapped up in their bedrolls, asleep. He crept up to the first cow thief and quickly slit his throat. The outlaw thrashed a little, but Jake held him down while watching the second one to see if he would wake up. When Jake was convinced that the first one was dead, he slipped over to the second outlaw, who was still fast asleep and snoring.

The night sky was cloudless. The countless stars and a full moon made enough light to see even the blood from the first man. Jake grabbed a fistful of hair and jerked the second man to an upright position. Jake pressed his knife to his throat as he hissed, "Can you see your pard?" The outlaw said shakily after seeing his partner lying in a pool of his own blood, "Yeah, I see him. Who the hell are you and what do you want?"

Jake twisted the man's head around slightly so he could see Jake's face painted black for war. The outlaw began sobbing and begging, "Please mister, don't kill me. You can have everythin' I got, just don't kill me."

Jake told him, "I only want one thing. I'm going to ask you one thing and you will only get one chance to give me an answer. If I don't like your answer, you and your pard will have matching throats."

The man pleaded, "Anythin' mister, I'll tell you anythin' you want to know."

Jake paused as he pressed the blade harder into the outlaw's throat. "I want to know where I can find Bloody Bill Clark, Frog Evans and Peg-leg Elliott." The rustler blurted out, "Hell mister, I can take you right to 'em, jest don't kill me!"

Jake mounted his horse as the outlaw saddled up. The outlaw led him to within a mile of Bloody Bill's camp. The outlaw pointed west and said, "Them boys you lookin' for are camped about a mile that-a-ways. I knowed where they was 'cause we been sellin' our cows to 'em."

Jake replied, "Mister, today is your lucky day. I'm going to let you live and I'm going to give you the chance to turn your life around. I want you to gather your gear and leave this part of the country. Find you an honest job and quit this life of thieving and killing. If you don't, one night you will wake up and I'll be there. There won't be any talking then, only dying. Do you understand me?"

The former outlaw said, "Yes sir, I will sir! You can count on me, sir!"

Jake tied up his horse to a Mesquite tree and crept up to the murderers' camp. He picked up a fist-sized rock and knocked each of them unconscious. When they came to, their hands were tied behind their backs and their feet were tied together. By now the sun was beginning to come up in the east. As each of them began to focus their cloudy vision, they saw Jake squatting by them with a look of cold hatred on his face. They weren't sure which was more terrifying, Jake being in war paint or the look in his eyes.

Jake spoke first. "Howdy boys, surprised to see me?"

Bloody Bill protested, "Now hold on, Jackson. We ain't done nothin'!"

Frog piped up, "Yeah, we don't have any idee who did that to your wife and kid!"

Jake replied, "Who said anything about my wife and child? How do you know something happened to them?"

Frog blustered, "Well we heared that somebody had kilt 'em."

Bloody Bill interrupted, "Shut up, Frog!"

Jake calmly started building a fire. Each man knew something terrible was about to be done to them but they didn't know what. Peg-leg was the first to break. "Mr. Jackson, Bill was the one who kilt your wife and kid! I didn't have nothing to do with it!"

Frog seconded Peg-leg. "It was Bill who did all the killin'. Me and Peg-leg had no part in the killin'."

Jake warmed himself by the fire and said, "Tell me something Frog, did you and Peg-leg take part in abusing my wife?"

Bloody Bill laughed, "Hell yes, they both took several turns. Hell, Frog was the first one to get on her."

As the outlaws continued denying their roles in the rape and murders, Jake thought in his mind what it must have been like for Macy Kathleen. He could visualize these animals attacking and killing her and Hunter. The thing that hurt the worst was he knew Macy Kathleen was expecting Jake to rescue her and the baby. The fact that he couldn't save them ate at him like a cancer deep in his bones.

Frog and Peg-leg begged and pleaded for their lives, but Bloody Bill was unrepentant. "Jackson, I can understand you're bein' upset bout losing your squaw. She was one fine piece of ass. But I did you a favor by gettin' rid of that squallin' kid. You should be thankin' me for that." Jake picked up the same rock that he used before and once more knocked the consciousness out of each of the men.

When they regained consciousness, Frog and Peg-leg found themselves still tied up but buried up to their necks with just their heads above ground. They felt something crawling on their heads and realized they had been planted next to a red ant bed. Jake squatted down next to them still in full war paint. He took his scalping knife and sawed off both men's eyelids. Frog and Peg-leg were screaming and begging, and their screams got even louder when Jake sliced off their scalps and threw them into the fire. As the blood poured down their faces and necks, the red ants must have rang the dinner bell. The insects began to swarm the two heads, feasting on their new-found food supply. Jake said in a calm voice, "I don't know how long it will take you boys to die. I guess however long it takes for those ants to eat you alive." Frog and Peg-leg screamed until they were hoarse and couldn't scream any more.

Fifty yards away, Bloody Bill hung by his hands from a live oak limb. His hands were tied together and his feet were tied together. He was far enough off the ground that he could just barely touch his toes to the ground. Bloody Bill was also naked, as Jake had stripped off all of his clothes.

Bloody Bill could see what Jake had done to Frog and Peg-leg. He was starting to lose all the bravado he had shown before. "Now Mr. Jackson, let's make some kind of deal. Do you want money? I got lots of money and can get more!" Jake stepped up to where his painted face was inches from the face of Macy Kathleen's and Hunter's killer. The cold look in Jake's eyes told Bloody Bill that he was doomed.

Jake scalped Bloody Bill, then made a six inch slice at the top of Bloody Bill's chest. He then slid the point of his knife just under the skin and began peeling it from Bloody Bill's body. Bloody Bill began to scream, cry and beg hysterically. Jake's face was cast in stone as he slowly skinned Bloody Bill alive. Jake stopped at his genitals, which he sliced off and stuffed in Bloody Bill's mouth. He didn't take any more skin from Bloody Bill. He didn't want him to die too fast. As it was, it still only took one day for all three men to die.

As Jake rode back to the Four Sixes, he knew that killing the men wouldn't bring back Macy Kathleen and Hunter but he felt that he had brought them some small measure of justice. As he rode under the night sky filled with brilliant, twinkling stars and further illuminated by a full, golden moon, Jake heard the lonely howl of a wolf. White Wolf took some consolation in listening to the wolf's howl. It was the Comanche way.

DRIFTER

———————

When he got to the ranch house, he told Burk, "It is finished. Macy Kathleen's and Hunter's killers are no longer breathing."

Burk didn't ask what happened to them because he didn't really want to know. He said, "Son, why don't you bunk tonight in the guest room. It really seems like it's your room anyway."

Burk had begun to think of Jake as a son. Jake replied, "Thanks, but I think I'll stay the night in the bunk house with the boys. I'm pushing on tomorrow and I want to say goodbye to them."

Burk asked, "Where you headed?"

Jake shrugged and said, "I'm not sure. I just know I need to travel and drift for a while."

The next morning after saying his goodbyes to Burk and the boys, Jake rode out to Billy's ranch to see him. As he and Billy stood by the graves of Macy Kathleen and Hunter, Billy said, "Jake, I got some things to do at the barn." They both knew that Billy was giving Jake some time alone at their graves.

Finally, Jake whispered to Macy Kathleen, "I know you're taking good care of Hunter. One day we will all be together again." With that, Jake went to the barn to say goodbye to Billy. For the rest of Billy's life, Jake would occasionally come to see him and visit their graves. Jake would always leave money on the kitchen table to help Billy out in his old age. Neither man ever mentioned the money to the other.

KID DALTON

J ake drifted from town to town. He knew how to live off the land and he had some money that Burk had insisted he take for the improvements on the ranch that he gave back to Burk.

One night Jake was in the Buckhorn Saloon in Mesquite, slowly sipping a whiskey when the "Kid" Dalton gang came in. The gang included "Good Time" Charlie Allen, George Alford and "Muleshoe" Frank Taggert. Dalton and his boys dumped a couple of the local cowboys out of their chairs so they could have their table.

Good Time Charlie was a functioning drunk. He got through life by staying drunk although most people couldn't tell that he was drunk. His constant need for alcohol required him to continually to be on the watch for something of value to steal to finance his habit. When Good Time Charlie needed a drink, he didn't care who he had to hurt to get it.

George Alford was a 300-pound serial rapist. He did not care whether his victims were young or old, fat or skinny, white, red, brown, yellow or black. George was incapable of any type of normal relationship. He was impotent if he was not forcing victims against their wills.

Muleshoe was just plain dumb. To say his intelligence was at the level of a mule was an insult to all mules. He got his nickname because his face bore a striking resemblance to a mule. Muleshoe's ears even flopped over at the top.

Kid Dalton was a killer. He had changed his name from Daniel Thompson to Kid Dalton at age thirteen to conceal his past. Kid certainly did not look like a killer. He stood only 5'5" and weighed 130 pounds. Daniel was small as a child and lived in fear of the other children as his stature always made him the low man on the totem pole. He was continually getting pushed around and beaten up, not only by the boys but also by some of the girls.

Daniel was babied by his mother Alice, because she felt sorry for him. He was ridiculed by his father Harry, who was ashamed of his diminutive son. Harry would say, "Boy, when are you gonna grow up and be a man? I never knowed anyone as chickenshit as you!" As Daniel would start to cry, Alice would rush to his side and smother him with hugs and kisses, saying to her husband, "Hush up, Harry. The poor baby can't help it if he's sensitive." As a young child, Kid's response to pretty much everything was to cry.

Everything changed when Daniel could no longer take the ridicule at school and at home. Something in him just snapped. The ten-year-old snuck his father's pistol out of the house and took it to school. He stood at the entrance to the little one-room schoolhouse and stoically shot and killed five of the other students and his teacher. After he ran out of bullets, he continued to point and dry-fire the gun. The witnesses who arrived on the scene in response to the screams of the surviving children said the boy seemed to be in a trance, and they had to force the pistol from his hand.

The parents of the dead children wanted to hang Daniel, but the general consensus of the community and the local sheriff was that you couldn't hang a ten-year-old boy. Harry and Alice were told by the sheriff to confine him to their small farm for his own good. Some of the men told Harry that, boy or no boy, if they ever saw Daniel again they would kill him.

Daniel never cried again for the rest of his life. Harry never ridiculed him again either, because he was now afraid of Daniel. Harry lived the next two years on pins and needles as he never knew when Daniel might go off again on another killing rampage. At the urging of Harry, Daniel finally left the farm in Mississippi, and under cover of night rode their old plowhorse to Texas. He had just turned twelve.

Daniel found a job at the Fletcher General Store in Kaufman. The owner of the store, Harold Fletcher, gave him a closet in the back of the store to sleep in. Harold fed him and gave him clothes and shoes that customers no longer wanted after buying new ones. Harold would only give them to Daniel if he thought he couldn't resell them.

Harold was a small, nervous man who always looked like he was on the verge of panicking. The only thing Harold didn't give Daniel was money. Harold told Daniel, "A boy your age don't need no money. I'm givin' you everythin' you need."

Daniel had worked at the general store for six months when two masked men tied their horses out back and kicked in the back door after the store had closed for the day.

Harold was at his house eating a home-cooked meal prepared by his greedy and nagging wife, Stella. Stella had unruly, frizzy orange hair. She was overweight from eating food that she kept hidden from Harold. Her eyebrows were also orange and were always arched in a questioning manner. Stella wasn't much of a cook but it beat having to fix something himself.

Harold had left Daniel at the store eating a sandwich consisting of a small slab of cheese between two stale slices of bread for his supper. Stella fixed two sandwiches for Harold to take to Daniel every day saying, "That damn kid don't need that much food cause he don't do shit! Sides, I need a new dress worser than he needs more food. I ain't had a new dress in over two weeks. I don't know why the hell I married you! My momma tried to warn me that I'd end up starvin' to death if I married you. Why in God's name didn't I listen to her? I'm just thankful my poor momma didn't live to see what my life has turned in to."

It had been years since the married couple had had sexual relations. This suited Harold fine as he would rather bed a female grizzly bear with a thorn in her paw then Stella.

When Stella's momma had passed away, she wailed like a banshee for a week. Harold was tired of her caterwauling after one day but did not possess large enough *cojones* to tell her to shut up. It took a Herculean effort from Harold not to break into an Irish jig whenever he thought about the old woman's death. While Stella's momma was a nightmare on two feet, the real horror to Harold was the snapshot of what Stella was going to be like in her old age.

One of the bandits grabbed Daniel by the front of his shirt, shoved his unshaven face and foul breath in Daniel's face and demanded, "Where's the money, boy?"

Daniel replied, "If I showed you where it is, will you take me with you and make me a part of yore gang?"

The second bandit laughed, "How 'bout you show us the money and to show how much I 'preciate it, I don't put a slug through yore stupid head."

Harold had tried to hide his secret stash of money. He especially didn't want Stella to know about it. Harold dreamed about saving enough money to leave the churlish Stella. He wanted to leave in the middle of the night and change his name so she could not find him.

Daniel had figured out that the money was in a false bottom of a box that was under the service counter. He fished the money out of the box and gave it to the two bandits. As they eagerly began to count it, Daniel remembered another secret stash of Harold's: his pistol. Daniel quietly pulled the gun and shot both distracted men in the back. The two outlaws had no idea that what looked like a little kid had already killed six people. Daniel knew that the gunshots were going to bring people to the store to see what was going on. He had only a minute to decide what to do. Daniel decided to take their horses, guns and the money and start a new life.

Fortunately for Daniel, the aborted robbery had taken place in a driving rainstorm. His escape was shielded by the rain washing out his tracks. A posse was formed to find Daniel but with no tracks to follow they finally gave up, as the situation was deemed hopeless.

Harold told the sheriff that Daniel had stolen some items from the store, but he was chagrined he couldn't tell the sheriff about the money because he didn't want Stella to know he had a hidden stash. When the posse came back empty-handed, Stella berated Harold, "That's what happens when you spoil someone like that kid! You was too nice to him. Momma was right, you are such a dumbass!"

Harold began to daydream about shooting, stabbing and strangling Stella to death. He wanted to do all three to eliminate any possibility of her surviving. Harold could imagine the smiling faces of the jury as the foreman read the verdict of not guilty by reason of justifiable homicide.

Daniel drifted, never stopping anywhere long enough for anyone to ask questions about him. At that point Daniel changed his name to Kid Dalton.

KID GROWS UP

Kid became a petty thief. His crimes were minor in nature until the day when he was caught untying another man's horse from a hitching rail. "Hold it! Where the hell do you think you're goin' with my horse?" shouted Big Ed Banion.

Kid had known that he would eventually get caught. He thought many times about what he would do when that happened. Kid replied, "I don't know what you're talkin' about. This here is my horse!"

Big Ed exploded, "Why you damn liar!" as he clumsily reached for his gun. Kid easily beat him to the draw and put two holes in his chest.

Since both Big Ed and Kid were strangers in town, no one knew who the real owner of the horse was. Several witnesses confirmed to the sheriff that Big Ed had gone for his gun first. It was a clear case of self-defense.

It occurred to Kid that he could take whatever he wanted if he could continue to play the self-defense card. In the past, Kid tried to make himself inconspicuous. After notching his first gunfight kill, he began to strut around like a little Banty rooster. Kid experienced an intoxicating high from killing Big

Ed. Kid wanted to kill more men. It was the best feeling that he ever had. No one could make fun of his size anymore. His gun made him as big as he wanted to be.

Kid's personality became larger than life. He attracted followers like Charlie, George and Muleshoe. Kid used his men to back his play in a gunfight. They could also be counted on to swear that the other man drew first. Kid no longer had to be concerned what witnesses would say. He had his own witnesses. When they divided up the spoils from a killing or robbery, Kid kept 75% and gave 10% to Charlie, 10% to George and 5% to Muleshoe. He told Muleshoe that he was getting an equal share. Muleshoe was too dumb to know the difference.

As Kid and his gang sat at the table at the Buckhorn throwing back shots of whiskey, Kid noticed Jake paying for his drink with a silver dollar. Kid whispered to his boys, "I think we got us a good un here," as he nodded toward Jake.

Kid stood up and walked over to stand across the table from Jake and said with a smirk, "Hey mister, do you know who I am?" Jake's gray eyes were expressionless as he replied, "No, can't say that I do. Am I supposed to know who you are?"

Kid exploded, "Everybody knows who I am!"

With that Charlie, George and Muleshoe got up and stood beside Kid, Muleshoe on his left, Charlie and George on his right. Jake took another drink of whiskey and calmly said, "It would be better for you to just tell me your name. I want to make sure the undertaker spells it right on your headstone."

Charlie was the first to go for his gun. From a seated position, Jake drew, fired and returned his gun to his holster before the rest of the men could move. Jake had shot off the top of Charlie's skull. Charlie's blood and brain matter had splattered the rest of the gang. Jake took another sip of whiskey. The look on his face was the same as if he had just swatted a fly.

Muleshoe was too dense to realize exactly what had just happened and he tried to draw his gun. Jake drew, shot and returned his gun to his holster before Kid or George could move. This time Jake's bullet entered the front of Muleshoe's throat and snapped his spine just below his head. Muleshoe's head flopped awkwardly to one side as he crumbled to the floor. Jake then nonchalantly took another sip of whiskey.

Sheer terror came over George as he never really saw Jake draw his gun. All he knew was somehow Jake shot Charlie and Muleshoe and it seemed that Jake's gun never left its holster. No one could ever remember seeing a 300-pound man move so fast as George sprinted out the door. As he ran, he made a high-pitched keening sound that scared most of the horses on the street. The townspeople George ran past in his pell-mell flight curled their noses in disgust as George had crapped his pants.

Kid was now alone facing Jake. He watched as Jake took another slow sip of whiskey. Jake said, "Looks like you've lost your army, general." Kid was desperately trying to think of an excuse to get out of the saloon but save face at the same time. A gunfighter like Kid could ill afford to have it said that he had backed down. Jake moved his hand to the whiskey bottle to pour himself another shot. The simple movement of Jake's hand startled Kid. He jumped backward, got his feet tangled and fell face-down flat on the floor.

The cowboys in the bar began to laugh. The more they laughed, the louder they laughed. Kid pushed off the floor and got to his feet. The laughter triggered his old disconnect. Kid no longer cared what happened to him. His sole purpose in life was to kill Jake and the men laughing at him.

Jake saw Kid's eyes change from being scared to becoming vacant. Jake knew that Kid had checked out emotionally. He knew that not being scared made Kid much more dangerous. Jake had seen Indian warriors check out of their bodies with the same blank stare. The ones who did that had no fear and would not stop until either they were dead or their enemy was dead.

Jake recalled Yellow Jacket going into that type of trance when their war party was returning from Buffalo Hump's great raid. Yellow Jacket then charged a band of Texas Rangers that were dug into a well-fortified position. Yellow Jacket must have been hit over a dozen times before falling off his horse.

As Kid went to draw his gun, Jake remained seated but drew both Peacemakers from their holsters. Jake was not going to take any chances with a man in Kid's state of mind. Jake riddled Kid with slugs. Kid was dead on his feet but his body stayed upright and continued to jerk as each bullet slammed into him.

Jake hung around long enough to tell the sheriff what had happened. His story was corroborated by the bartender and the other patrons.

THE SLICK
KING GANG

J ake's legend continued to grow with each gunfight. Jake just wanted to be left alone. He had no desire to be famous but it seemed he couldn't escape his fate.

Slick King made his first trip to prison at the ripe old age of sixteen, for rustling cows. He quickly learned in prison that only the ruthless survived. Slick had a well-deserved reputation for being a hardened bandit and killer. He stood out from the crowd with his brightly colored clothes and his double-rig, ivory-handled pistols.

He once gunned down three members of his own gang over a question regarding a split of the loot from a bank heist. The gang members were concerned about Slick's counting skills. When it came time to divvy up the money, Texas Jack Reed said, "Boss, me and the boys thought there was gonna be more money than that." Slick grinned and replied, "You boys agree with ol' Jack here?" When the other two outlaws nodded their heads, Slick resolved their math question with a bullet to the heart of each man.

It was said that Slick slaughtered a Mexican family of five, including a father, mother and three young boys, because their burro-pulled cart had taken up too much of the road. He gunned down the adults and killed the screaming boys with his knife. As Slick, covered in blood, remounted his horse, he reportedly said, "Damn pepper bellies! The world will be better off when they're all dead."

The five members of his gang that were riding with him were all hard cases, killers and thieves, but this took the brutality they were familiar with to a whole new level.

Slick began to enlarge his gang. He had an insane vision of owning all of Texas and being its king. His gang included One-eye Miller, whom everyone though was going to meet his demise at the hands of a lynch mob one night. With the rope snug around his neck and standing on a box, waiting for it to get kicked out from under him, One-eye took matters into his own hands by saying, "Let 'er rip!" as he jumped off the box. The rope snapped, allowing some of One-eye's buddies to shoot into the surrounding crowd, letting One-eye escape to safety.

Mexican Pete joined Slick's gang. He began his murderous career by stabbing a fellow classmate to death in the schoolyard at the age of 14. Slick overlooked Pete's Mexican heritage because Pete would ruthlessly follow any order given by King.

Apache Jack, a Mescalero Apache whose own people banned him from their tribe for repeated murders and thefts, was another valuable member of Slick's gang.

Slick recruited Curley Bill Bennett, who was a notorious gunman, cattle rustler and horse thief. Curley Bill once invited a man to supper. At the end of the meal, Curley Bill drew his pistol and shot the man between the eyes. When asked why he would invite someone to supper and then kill him, Curley Bill said, "I hate to send a man to Hell on an empty stomach."

These four blights on humanity were to become King's lieutenants, each in charge of eight to ten soldiers. The total number of men in the gang fluctuated from thirty to forty, depending on who got killed that week and how long it took to recruit a replacement.

Some white men wouldn't work under a Mexican like Pete or an Indian like Jack. Two new recruits were brought before Slick. Slick told them, "Jeb, you'll be workin' fer Mexican Pete, and Dave, you'll be working' fer Apache Jack."

Jeb retorted, "The hell I will! I ain't working fer no damn Messican!"

Dave joined in, "I'll be damned if I work fer no Injun!" Slick resolved their objections to their new bosses by shooting them both in the head. Word got around. There were no more complaints about job assignments.

The gang covered the spectrum of crimes: bank robbery, stagecoach hijacking, kidnapping, rape, murder-for-hire and extortion. Nothing was off limits for this collection of the dregs of society.

Another gang member of note was Slick's girlfriend, Lori Schuett. Lori didn't consider herself a gang member. If Slick thought of himself as the king, Lori thought of herself as the queen. She was from a family German immigrants. There were a number of unexplained gruesome deaths of neighbors, including corpses that had been filleted like catfish, and others burned beyond recognition. When all signs pointed to Lori, Lori's father and mother packed up all of her things and dropped off the sixteen-year-old in Cleburne, the nearest town.

Lori's father said, "Here is ten dollars. If you come back to the farm, I will shoot you on sight."

Lori shot a glance at her mother, but her mother just shuddered and turned away desperately, saying, "Let's go, Pa!"

The last thing they heard as they drove the buckboard away was Lori's maniacal laugh. She thought it was hysterical that her parents were scared to death of her. In fact, she was very pleased with herself.

At a distance, Lori looked like a normal woman, but she was every bit as insane as Slick—some would say even more so. She had a look in her eyes that would unnerve most sane people. At times, even Slick was a little nervous around her. Lori's creepy laugh was the loudest when others were suffering the most.

When Slick suffered a gunshot wound in his left calf during a holdup, Lori examined it by digging her fingers into his bleeding flesh. She cackled, "Does this hurt?" Slick looked at her nervously when she doubled over with laughter.

Slick shared his bed with her but would not go to sleep until they were finished and he had locked her in another bedroom. Even though he always double-checked the lock, many nights he woke in a cold sweat and screaming from a nightmare about Lori skinning him like a fish or setting him on fire. In the dream, Slick would beg Lori to put out the fire. She responded by throwing coal oil on him. And regardless of how she would be torturing him, all the nightmares had one thing in common: her incessant, maniacal laughter. Most unnerving of all was that her laugh in the nightmare was the same as it was in real life.

Curley Bill and his band of eight outlaws from the King gang were waiting for the stagecoach to change horses at the Buzzard Pass depot. They didn't bother to wear masks because they wanted everyone to know who they were. Slick's goal was to have everyone terrified of his gang.

Curley Bill and his boys galloped out of their hiding spot in the nearby brush and quickly surrounded the stage and depot. The guard for the stage reached for his shotgun and was promptly riddled with a barrage of bullets for his trouble. Even after it was evident that he was dead, the outlaws continued to pump bullets into his lifeless body because it entertained them to see the corpse dance.

Curley Bill shouted, "Git down from that stage, driver. Everybody out of the stage!" As he and his men dismounted, three passengers stepped out. They were Ed Rush, a banker, his wife Martha, and their thirteen-year-old daughter Mary. After one of his men had collected their valuables, Curley Bill shot and killed Ed, saying, "That's just to let you know I'm serious. Driver, iffen you don't give me any problems, I will let you live to tell that you wuz robbed by Curley Bill and the Slick King Gang." Then Curley Bill turned to the two women saying, "Now you wimmen give me and my boys what we want and you might live too."

Two of his men grabbed the terrified and crying woman and girl, bent them over a hitching rail as they pushed their skirts and petticoats over their heads. They ripped their undergarments off as the other outlaws began undoing their gun belts and dropping their pants.

Curley Bill held his gun on the driver. Flatnose Ketchum announced, "I'm goin' first! The rest of you jackasses are behind me!"

The stagecoach line, Butterfield Express, had hired Jake to put an end to the stage robberies they were suffering at the hands of the King gang. Jake had just recently received a tip regarding the general location of the gang.

Jake had picked up the trail of the outlaws earlier that day and was just now arriving at the scene of the murder and gang rape. He quickly sized up the situation and urged Hellfire into his fastest gallop. The outlaws didn't see him coming until it was too late. Bullets from his Peacemakers killed seven of the outlaws immediately. He made sure that Flatnose was the first to die because he was the first in line.

The eighth, Jasper Tucker, had a bullet hole in his upper chest as he pulled Mary in front of him as a shield. Jasper held his knife to Mary's throat and said, "Back off, Jackson, or I'll cut this little girl's throat from one of her pretty little ears to the other." Jasper peered around Mary's head with only his right eye showing. One of Jake's Peacemakers barked. The bullet punched through Jasper's eye and exited out of the back of his head.

In the meantime, Curley Bill had used the hostage situation to mount his horse and high-tail it out of there. His right arm was dangling, as one of Jake's bullets had broken it.

When Curley Bill made it back to the outlaw camp to tell Slick how Jake Jackson had stopped the holdup of the stage, Slick began ranting and raving about Jake. "I want that son of a bitch dead! And, I want him to die slow! I want him to take a week in dying and I want to be there to watch! I want him to know it was Slick King that brought down the great, high and mighty Jake Jackson. I want him to beg for his life! If he has any friends, I want them dead too!" Slick was starting to slobber, but none of his men wanted to point that out to him.

Later, Slick walked up to Curley Bill as he was trying to put his broken arm in a sling and said, "You ain't worth a piss!" and blew the top of Curley Bill's head off. "The rest of you galoots best do your damn jobs. I won't have nobody in my gang that can't git it done." Pointing at the exposed brain in Curley Bill's skull that was now mush, he said, "That will be your last pay iffen you don't do your job!" Slick started to laugh. Even the most hardened of the gang members felt a shiver go up their spine.

THE GENERAL

Geneeral George Montgomery had served in the Army headquarters in Washington, D.C. for thirty years. He began as a second lieutenant and rose through the ranks to general. Along the way, he developed a reputation for honesty and integrity. He was a man you could ride the river with.

When he retired, he bought 60,000 acres in South Texas and established the Willow Creek Ranch. With his connections, the General knew he could make a fortune raising cattle and selling them to the army. He built the largest home in the entire southwest. He stocked his ranch with cheap cattle from Mexico and hired a crew to manage the herd and the ranch.

General Montgomery only made one mistake. His crew were cowboys who knew everything about cattle, but they weren't gun hands. As he gradually started to lose more and more of his herd to rustlers, the General realized his cowboys were no match for the hardened criminals of the Slick King Gang. Slick even killed other rustlers who were trying to steal the General's cows. He claimed the General's herd as his own. The General made up his mind to take action after more cattle were driven off and two of his cowboys were found dead after being ambushed.

The General called his ranch foreman, Slim Whitman, into his office and said, "Slim, I want you to take a ride up to Ft. Worth to the Deadwood Saloon. Ask for the owner, Andy Fincher. I want you to give him this note and a hundred dollars in gold. Tell Fincher the note is for Jake Jackson and the gold is for Jake's expenses to come meet with me." Andy and the Deadwood had become the message center for anyone wanting to reach Jake.

Slim was a tall, thin cowboy whose legs were bowed after a lifetime in the saddle. After Slim delivered the note and the gold, Andy told everybody who came in that if they saw Jake to tell him that Andy had something for him.

The General only had one child, his daughter Allison. His wife Sophie had died giving birth to her. The General doted on her. He couldn't help spoiling her even with his military background. Allison was a beautiful child with curly blond hair and striking, green eyes. The hardest decision that he ever made was to send Allison to be educated in England. He made the long trip by ship every year to visit her. Allison completed her education by graduating from Cambridge.

The General made the long trip once again for Allison's graduation. After the graduation ceremonies, Allison said to her father, "General (she had always called him General even as a child), I want to come live on your ranch in Texas."

The General replied, "Allison, dearest, I cannot allow that because that country is still wild and untamed. It is much too dangerous."

Allison said, "But General, I want to be closer to you. I hate life here in England. It is all so... predictable. I want some adventure!"

The General chuckled. "Allison, sweetheart, I wish that it was safe for you at the ranch. I would love to be able to see you every day instead of once a year. Also, you have a higher quality of potential husbands here. Who would you marry in Texas, some cowboy?"

Allison retorted, "Well, I'm damn sure not going to marry one of these damn Englishmen. They are so polite and courteous, they drive me up a wall!"

The General was shocked. "Allison Montgomery, you watch your tongue! A lady does not use that kind of language!"

While the rebellious Allison nodded her head to pacify her father, she thought to herself, *I don't want to be a damn lady, either.*

After the General set sail to return to America, Allison gathered all her things and two weeks later caught the next ship heading to New York.

The General had been back at the ranch for almost three weeks when he saw a buckboard coming down the road to his massive house. Allison had taken a second ship from New York to Galveston. She had bought a buckboard and horses and hired two ex-Texas Rangers to escort her to the General's ranch. Both men came highly recommended by the sheriff in Galveston. Sheriff "Big Mike" Green told Allison, "Rube Burrow and 'Shotgun Johnny' Johnson are fine men and will see you safely to your father's ranch. I have met the General on several occasions. Be sure to give him my regards."

When the General realized it was Allison, he ran from the porch to embrace her. He then held her at arm's length to make sure she was all right and said, "Allison, what in the world are you doing here? Have you taken leave of your senses?"

Allison replied, "General, I am a grown woman. I will have a say where I will live. Right now, my place is with you." The General just shook his head, not knowing what to do with her.

Allison continued, "These two gentlemen are Mr. Johnson and Mr. Burrow. They are ex-Texas Rangers. "Big Mike" Green said they could be trusted to bring me safely to the ranch. He also told me to tell you hello."

The General greeted the men. "Gentlemen, thank you for seeing my daughter home safely. If you have no other jobs on the horizon, I would like to hire you to protect her."

Shotgun Johnny said, "Shore, General, we would like to work here at yore ranch. Big Mike said you was a fine feller." The General called Slim over to get Johnny and Rube settled in to the bunk house.

The next day, Jake rode up to the main house to see the General. Slim had seen Jake coming and notified the General. The General was waiting on the front porch to greet Jake. He stuck out his hand and said, "Mr. Jackson, I'm General Montgomery. It was good of you to come."

Jake shook his hand as he replied, "General, it's a pleasure. I have only heard good things about you so I wanted to hear what you had to say."

Allison came out of the door on to the porch. The General introduced her. "Mr. Jackson, this is my daughter, Allison." Jake tipped his hat and politely said, "Ma'am."

Slim interjected as he eyed Hellfire, "Mr. Jackson, what do you want me to do with your horse?" The big stud was famous throughout the Southwest. Some of the cowboys were already gathered around to admire Hellfire. Slim was perplexed, as Hellfire didn't have anything on him that he could use to tie him up.

Jake smiled, "He's really not my horse. You don't have to do anything with him. He's free to come and go as he pleases." One of the cowboys said in a low voice, "I ain't never heared of such. This just beats all."

The General asked Jake to come into the parlor. He asked Allison to excuse them. The look on Allison's face clearly said she was not pleased about being dismissed. The General invited Jake to sit down after ordering two cups of coffee from his cook, Millie. He then closed the door, much to the aggravation of Allison as she had hoped she would at least be able to eavesdrop.

The General began, "Mr. Jackson..."

Jake interrupted, "General, please call me Jake."

The General continued, "Jake, I'm sure you know that the Slick King Gang is a thorn in my side. I haven't been able to stop them from rustling my cattle. They've even killed a couple of my men. I've thought about calling in the Army, but they are already spread too thin in this part of Texas. This is where you come in. I need someone like yourself to stop this bunch of thieves. I need a professional who will take whatever steps are necessary to get the job done."

Millie had fixed the coffee and was bringing the tray when she was intercepted by Allison. "Here Millie, I'll take that."

Millie protested, "But Miss Allison, the General clearly told..."

At that point Allison forcibly took the tray from Millie saying, "Don't worry dear. It will be all right."

Allison opened the parlor door and swept into the room carrying the tray, making a grand entrance. "Gentlemen, here is your coffee. I know you menfolk aren't much good without your coffee."

After her father and Jake took their cups off the tray, Allison set the tray on a small table and plopped down on a couch. Jake was amused but the General was not. He raised an eyebrow and gave Allison a questioning look.

Allison responded, "Now don't y'all pay any attention to little ol' me. Just think of me as a fly on the wall."

General looked at Jake. "As you can see, I have somewhat spoiled my daughter. She was educated in England but evidently wasn't paying attention during her classes on etiquette. Do you mind if she stays?"

Jake laughed, "No sir, I don't object at all."

The General continued, "Jake, if you can rid me of this gang of thieves and killers, I will pay your expenses plus $10,000 in gold when they're... disposed of, if you get my drift."

Allison was shocked. She interrupted, "General, are you hiring this man to kill those outlaws?"

The General angrily said, "Allison, I have let you stay against my better judgment, but I don't want to hear your opinions about something you know nothing about! Anything else out of you and I will insist that you leave." Allison was not used to her father speaking to her in that harsh of a tone. She decided to shut up.

Jake spoke to Allison, "Miss Montgomery, Texas is not England. The law here sometimes has to be enforced by a gun. Please remember that these men have stolen your cattle and killed your men. I will give them a chance to surrender and be given a fair trial. Frankly, I have dealt with these types of men all my life. There is a zero chance they will choose to be tried in court. Their choice most likely will be to try to kill me."

After taking a few minutes to think it over as Jake and her father watched her, she said, "Mr. Jackson, I can sense that you are an honest man and you are telling me the truth. Make no mistake, I am my father's daughter. If the choice comes down to them or you, I say kill them."

Jake started patrolling Willow Creek and caught the Slick King Gang stealing cows on two different occasions. Each time Jake had to kill the rustlers. He killed three the first time and killed another four the second time.

When his men did not comeback, Slick sent a couple of his other men to see what happened to them. They came back with a report after the first time that they had not found the men but did find three graves. They report for the second time was the same but there were four graves.

Slick was ranting and raving, "How the hell did I git such a big bunch of wimmen workin' for me? Ain't nobody got enough balls to kill this damn Jackson?"

Apache Jack spoke up. "Boss, I can kill the bastard and I got me a plan on just how to do it."

Allison began to have a secret attraction to Jake. Even though Jake was 35 years older than Allison, she didn't see him as a father figure. She saw that he didn't have an ounce of fat on his muscular frame and she couldn't help staring at Jake's gray eyes. Her infatuation with Jake got so bad that Allison started daydreaming about the day she and Jake would get married. But Jake had not been interested in another woman since Macy Kathleen and Hunter were murdered.

Allison had learned to ride in England and had developed a love for riding horses. The General gave her a gentle strawberry-roan filly. Slim had picked her out especially for Allison. Slim told the General, "This little filly is so gentle even a kid could ride her." Allison named her Scarlet. Allison loved Scarlet and couldn't wait to go on a long ride with her every day.

Allison was accompanied on her daily rides by Johnny and Rube. The days stretched into weeks and the boys let their guard down. They didn't see the glint off the rifle barrels. They didn't even hear the shots. Allison panicked as Johnny and Rube were blown out of their saddles. She pivoted Scarlet in the direction of the ranch house and put her heels into the horse. Scarlet was in an all-out gallop when two horsemen jumped out of the brush in front of her. One of the men grabbed Scarlet's reins.

Allison shouted, "Let me go! My father will hang you for this!"

Apache Jack rode up to her and said, "We ain't none too worried about your damn daddy. After we take care of Jackson, your daddy's gonna git what's comin' to him." They drug Scarlet by the reins with Allison still in the saddle back to their camp. As they tied her up, Apache Jack had a big grin as he groped her body, squeezing anything he wanted to. Seeing Jack take his liberties, several of the other men joined in. They ripped open her shirt and exposed her breasts. Allison started spitting and trying to bite them, "You're not men! You're animals! The General will send Jake Jackson to get me! Jake will make you wish you had never been born."

Lori watched the men manhandle Allison, laughing like the maniac she was. She hardly spoke in complete sentences any more. Her descent into total madness was accompanied by the laughter that made everyone within earshot cringe in horror.

Slick called a halt to the assault. "That's enough, boys. To git what we want, we might have to show she ain't been hurt too bad. We want the General to pay whatever it takes to git Jackson to come git her." Slick told one of his men to bring Scarlet out. Allison was already terrified and had a knot in the pit of her stomach that something worse was going to happen.

Slick pulled his pistol and shot Scarlet. The horse squealed as she went down. Scarlet kicked a few times and then died.

Allison was screaming and sobbing hysterically. "Nooooooo! Nooooo! Why? Why would you do that?"

Slick just snickered, "That's just to let you know who's runnin' things here. I decide who lives or who dies."

Slick wouldn't let his men touch her anymore, but he didn't stop them from stripping her naked. He let them look all they wanted. Allison was totally humiliated.

Johnny's and Rube's horses galloped up to the barn. Slim caught them and went to the house to report to the General. Slim shouted, "General! General! The horses that Johnny and Rube was ridin' just showed up at the barn, and there's blood on the saddles!"

The General grabbed his arm. "What about Allison?"

Slim replied, "There's no sign of her!"

The General ordered, "Send ten men to back trail the boys' horses. I want you to take a couple of men and go find Jake."

The General's men found the bodies of Johnny and Rube. Pinned to Rube's shirt was a note that said, "Jackson, if you want to see this little bitch of the General's alive again, meet me at the little clearing next to Bald Knob at daylight. I hope you ain't scairt to come. If you don't, I will cut her up into little pieces and send her back to the General, one piece at a time." It was signed by Slick King. Slick planned on skinning Jake alive and tacking his hide to the barn door at their hideout.

Slim had a good idea where to find Jake and brought him back at a gallop to the ranch house. Jake read the note. The General was worried sick about Allison. He asked Jake, "Why aren't they asking for a ransom?"

Jake replied, "Because King doesn't want money. All he wants right now is to kill me. And if he can kill me, you will be next."

The General said desperately, "Jake, what are you planning on doing?"

Jake responded, "I plan on meeting this crazy son of a bitch in the morning at Bald Knob."

The General pleaded, "Please rescue her. I will pay you anything you want."

Jake put his hand reassuringly on the General's trembling shoulder. "General, if I can save Allison, I would never take any money for that. It is the right thing to do."

Jake entered the clearing near Bald Knob where he was supposed to meet the outlaws. He could see the ten outlaws led by Apache Jack. Jake could also see Allison tied to a tree naked behind them with Laughing Sam Slade holding his gun to her head. When Laughing Sam pulled Allison off her horse to tie her to the tree, Allison did her best to wipe the stupid grin off his face with a well-places kick to his crotch. Laughing Sam grunted from her kick, then slapped Allison hard enough to knock her down. Sam told her as he roughly tied her to the tree, "I hope you're that feisty later on. I like my wimmin feisty."

Jake slowly started to walk Hellfire toward the gang. The outlaws pointed their pistols and rifles at Jake. They were concerned even though they knew they had him dead to rights. What puzzled them was why he would deliberately ride to his own death. Jake didn't seem like he had a care in the world. With the slightest touch of his legs from Jake, Hellfire was at full speed in two strides, charging the outlaws. Bullets whistled through the sleeves of his shirt. One bullet creased his side, cutting a narrow furrow about six inches long. Another bullet went through the crown of his Stetson, knocking his hat off his head. Jake roared, "Damn you! That was my favorite hat!"

Jake had filled his hands with his Peacemakers, firing with both as he passed through the line of outlaws. After his first pass through, six outlaws were dead on the ground, including Laughing Sam Slade, who was the first one to die as he was assigned to kill Allison if there were any problems. Otherwise, they planned on taking her back to camp to be used by whoever wanted her as many times as they wanted her.

Jake's very first shot was at 75 yards from one of his pistols. He had targeted Laughing Sam. Laughing Sam lived up to his name by laughing out loud at Jake firing from such a great distance saying, "What is that dern fool..." Laughing Sam's laugh and his voice were erased by a .45 caliber slug that tore out his throat. It seemed that Jake had the last laugh.

Hellfire's bloodlust was up as the big stud wheeled and ran over one of the remaining outlaw's horses, knocking the horse to the ground and causing his rider to break his neck in the fall. The last three outlaws were on the ground, having been bucked off their horses by the barrage of gunfire from the riders shooting from their backs with their guns firing inches from the horses' ears.

Apache Jack and the other two outlaws had emptied their guns and were too afraid to take the time to reload as Jake and Hellfire seemed to move faster than their eyes could follow. Instead, they drew their knives and were in a crouch that was familiar to experienced knife fighters such as themselves.

Jake pulled his scalping knife and rode past Apache Jack, making a downward slash. Apache Jack's nose, along with half of his face, pitched into the dirt at his feet. His body toppled over following his nose.

Jake leapt from Hellfire's back and approached the last two knife fighters. They circled Jake trying to gain an advantage. As soon as Big Foot Newcomb got behind him, he thrust his knife at Jake's back. Jake anticipated Big Foot's move and whirled, slashing with his knife. The outlaw's knife hand was severed at the wrist. He grabbed his stump and fell to the ground moaning and bawling. Big Foot cried pitifully, "Momma, help me!" as the stump pumped blood in long spurts.

Jake and the other outlaw ignored his pleas. Big Foot had never shown mercy to any of his many victims. He should have known none would be shown to him. No one cared that he bled to death.

The last outlaw, Bitter Creek Reynolds, bent down and grabbed a handful of dirt to throw in Jake's eyes. Before he could blind Jake, Jake threw his knife end over end, thudding into Bitter Creek's chest. The knife was buried up to its handle.

Allison was crying and red-faced with shame at her nakedness in front of Jake. Jake pretended not to notice as he cut her loose, wrapped her in a blanket confiscated from one of the outlaw's saddle and mounted her on one of their horses. Jake then scalped all ten of the outlaws and stuffed the bloody hair into a saddlebag on the saddle of Allison's horse. When Allison looked at him with horror, Jake said, "Allison, you now know firsthand the kind of men we're dealing with. I have to send Slick King a message that he will understand." On the ride back to the ranch, Allison was sniffling. Jake softly asked, "How bad did they hurt you?"

Allison knew what he was asking. "No, they didn't rape me, but they did everything else but that!" Allison's slowly falling tears became a torrent as she convulsed in great, racking sobs.

Jake stopped Hellfire and slid off him. He pulled Allison down from her saddle and held her. Jake stroked her hair soothingly. "I know what a shock this has been for you. I know you feel like your world has come to an end. Right now, you just cry until you don't want to cry anymore. I know you can't see it now, but one day you will realize that it could have been a lot worse." Allison cried for the better part of an hour.

Finally, she looked at Jake and said, "Okay, I think I'm done. Please take me home."

The General cried with joy when Jake rode in with Allison safe and sound. The cowboys who were at the ranch that day clapped and cheered. The General put his arm around the still distraught Allison and guided her into the house. Millie brought her some hot tea as Allison poured out her story of pain and humiliation. Millie cried throughout the telling of her story. At the end of the story, the General was in a killing rage.

Outside, Slim and the other hands came up to Jake shaking his hand and slapping his back. Slim asked Jake, "What happened out there?"

Jake reluctantly replied, "Well, let's just say that the only ones who made it out alive were Allison and me." This prompted the men to slap his back even harder as they expressed their admiration.

The General was visibly upset as he came out on the porch and said, "Jake, Allison told me what you did. I am a veteran of several wars and I don't know that I've ever heard of that kind of bravery before. You can have anything that I've got as a reward for saving my daughter. You name it and it's yours!"

Jake answered, "General, that's a mighty kind offer but I only did my duty. Thanks, but I already have everything that I need."

JOHNNY
CONCHO

After a couple of days, Jake rode to Ft. Worth with the ten outlaw scalps. He nailed the scalps to one of the walls at the Deadwood Saloon. Jake also nailed up a sign that said,

> *To: Slick King*
>
> *Here are the remains of some of your men.*
>
> *You can come collect them at any time.*
>
> *What's left of them has already been claimed by coyotes and buzzards.*

Of course, this news spread like wildfire. The saloon stayed packed with people coming from all over wanting to see the scalps. After Jake's last two visits to his saloon, he became a welcome sight to Andy. Now when Andy saw Jake, he saw dollar signs. Jake let Slick King know that not only could Jake fight fire with fire but he could also fight terror with terror.

Jake had killed a large number of the King Gang. Slick knew he couldn't continue to take such heavy losses. He was crazy, but he wasn't stupid. He sent One-eye Miller and two of his men to Austin with $5,000 in gold to fetch Johnny Concho.

On the ride to Austin, One-eye and his men were thinking the obvious. One-eye said, "Boys, what would keep us from splittin' this money and just keep on ridin'?"

After a period of silence, one of the other men replied, "To hell with that! I ain't crossin' Slick. That son of a bitch would send every one of his men after us. Might as well put a gun to our heads and blow out our brains right here."

One-eye laughed, "He would probably have to empty his gun to find yore brain, but I reckon you're right. We'd have to spend the rest of our lives lookin' over our shoulder. I'd rather have those damn Pinkertons on my trail than Slick."

One-eye and his boys found Johnny Concho at the Texican Saloon in Austin. Concho was sitting at a corner table sipping on a whiskey. Johnny just sipped his whiskey and spaced out his drinks because he wanted to be alert enough to gun someone down if the need arose.

One-eye said to Johnny, "Me and the boys brung you this sack of gold but you have to come with us to meet with our boss, Slick King. The boss said to tell you that he had a little job for you. Iffen you can do it, Slick said there's more gold in it for you."

Concho dumped out the contents of the sack on the table. He looked up at One-eye and said, "I like yore boss's style. I reckon this will pay for the ride to yore camp. But, you best not be shittin' me about more gold. I wouldn't take kindly to that."

As they got in the general vicinity of the outlaws' nest, One-eye nervously said, "From here on in we're gonna have to blindfold you. The boss don't like folks knowin' where our camp is."

Concho belched a sinister laugh. "You take that blindfold and stick it up yore ass!"

Everyone knew of the notorious Johnny Concho. He had killed over fifty men in gunfights. Concho took on all comers. His quick draw was only rivaled by Jake Jackson. Most people still gave the edge to Jake, but nobody dared to tell Concho that.

No one knew that his real name was Jonathan Farmer, the son of an itineran fire-and-brimstone preacher. His father told anyone and everyone that they were going to Hell.

Jonathan left home at age fourteen. He could no longer tolerate his daily Bible lesson that was applied across his back with a green branch from the peach tree next to the sod house as his father shouted, "The Good Book says, 'Spare the rod and spoil the child!' I'm doin' this for your own good, boy! You don't want the Devil to git you, do you?"

Jonathan said goodbye to his father by slitting his throat as he slept. For good measure, he also cut his mother's throat for allowing him to be abused by his father.

Jonathan buried his parents not out of respect for them but because he wanted to hide his crime. He was pretty sure that they would not be missed, but wanted to be on the safe side by putting them under the dirt. As he stood over the fresh graves, he pulled off his hat and said, "I reckon the decent thing to do is say some words... I hope you both burn in Hell!" He put everything of value, which wasn't much, in an old burlap bag and mounted their old mule, Bones, who came by his name honestly. Jonathan left Alabama and went west.

In Louisiana his luck went from bad to worse. He fell in with a couple of killers named Ike and Sawyer. They never told anyone their last names because they were wanted in two states. The men welcomed Jonathan, saying they would treat him like their son. Ike put his arm around Jonathan and said, "I always wanted to have me a son."

The very first night, they sexually assaulted the young, thin boy. This went on for about a week, until one night Jonathan took advantage of their drunken stupor and calmly cut their throats. He didn't bother to bury them. He was in too big of a hurry to leave.

Jonathan was considerably richer as he now had their guns, horses and provisions. He was tired of being abused. Jonathan didn't want to ever have to wait again until his abusers were vulnerable to his knife. He wanted to stop any attack before it started. He swore that no one would ever abuse him again.

Jonathan began practicing with the guns and the ample ammo that he confiscated from Ike and Sam. He found that he was a natural. In less than a month, he became an accomplished quick-draw artist and an exceptional shot. Jonathan had a knack for guns. He was all of fourteen.

Then came the day that Jonathan was walking on the wooden sidewalk in Kaufman, Texas. Rip Vernon and his buddy Satch Faris watched this kid with two guns strapped to his legs. As he stepped in front of Jonathan, Rip said, "Well looky here. We got us a real bad man. Boy, where'd you git them big ole guns?"

Jonathan stopped, but didn't say a word. Satch, who was leaned up against a hitching rail, added, "Boy, my pard asked you a damn question. You best answer him or we'll take those big guns away and tan your hide with em." Rip and Satch laughed at the thought of whuppin this snot-nosed kid's ass with his own guns.

Even though Jonathan looked exactly like what he was, a fourteen-year-old kid, he moved his hands to hover over the handles of his pistols. There was a coldness in his eyes as he said, "Mister, you need to move yore ass out of my way while you still can."

By now a crowd had gathered, expecting to see the kid get hurrahed by the men. Satch jumped off the hitching rail and stood side by side with Rip as he threatened, "Boy, you're damn close to gittin' yourself killed, kid or no kid. You move your hands any closer to them guns and I'm gonna blow you off this here sidewalk."

Jonathan replied, "You two old peckerwoods need to git out of my way or draw."

Rip said, "Why you little son of a bitch!" as he started to pull his pistol. It happened so fast that the bystanders weren't quite sure what happened next. They all agreed that the kid must have jerked both guns from their holsters but it happened so quick that no one actually saw his draw. His guns just appeared in his hands. Jonathan fired before either man had gotten their guns halfway out of their holsters. Rip and Satch fell stone dead.

Bystanders disagreed about how many shots Jonathan fired. Some said two, some said just one. The four shots were so rapid that it seemed the sound was just one or two at the most. Everyone did finally agree on one thing: Rip and Satch had four bullet holes where their eyes used to be.

Jonathan went through their pockets, confiscating their cash. No one challenged him regarding his right to the money. Jonathan went into the dry goods store and bought a shiny black vest that was decorated with silver conchos. As he stepped back out on the sidewalk, someone said, "What's yer name kid?" Jonathan turned and slowly said, "John…ny….Concho, Johnny Concho." That was the beginning of the legend that was Johnny Concho.

When they rode into camp, One-eye said to Concho, "Stay here and lemme go git the boss." One-eye then scurried into one of the buildings that served as a saloon from the once-deserted ghost town.

Slick was sitting at a table shuffling cards. One-eye said, "Boss, I brung him like you said. And I told him that he should wear the blindfold but he wouldn't do it."

Slick asked, "Whad he say 'bout the blindfold?"

One-eye hemmed and hawed, "Well… he… sorta… told me to stick it up my ass."

Slick exploded in laughter. "Good! I wouldn't expected someone like him to take orders from the likes of you."

Johnny got off his horse and strutted around the camp like he owned the place. He was a hero to most of the other outlaws. Johnny could see the admiration in their eyes. They wanted to be like Johnny Concho, respected but mostly feared.

Mexican Pete said under his breath, "This gringo don't look so tough to me."

Johnny turned to him and said, "If you got somethin' to say, Mex, spit it out. I don't know why you're a part of this gang noways. Every Messican I ever knowed was yellow when the fightin' started."

Mexican Pete bristled at the insult and moved his hand closer to the handle of his pistol as he said, "Hijo de puta, maybe we find out who is yellow?"

Slick walked up and said, "That's enough, Pete! I got plans for Mr. Concho here. I don't speck he could do what I need him to do iffen you was to ventilate him."

Concho snorted, "That ain't never gonna happen. This Messican of yourn wouldn't have time to piss in his pants before he would be tamale meat."

Slick and Johnny went back in the makeshift saloon and sat down at the table. After eyeing each other a bit, Slick said, "I gotta job fer you. I want you to kill Jake Jackson. Are you man enough to do that?"

Johnny smirked, "I can kill whoever I damn well please. But why should I want to kill him?"

Slick leaned back in his chair, "Cause I got another $20,000 in gold fer you iffen you do."

Johnny pulled out a thin cigar and began chewing on it as he studied Slick. "Why do you need me? Why don't you have one on them dry-gulchers who works for you kill him?"

Slick responded, "I done already sent three of my best men to do exactly that. Not a one come back. Ain't nobody seen or heard from 'em agin. I knowed Jackson kilt 'em."

Slick poured whiskey for both men. After several shots apiece, Slick said, "Well, Concho, what's it gonna be? You gonna gun Jackson or not?"

Johnny mulled it over for a few more minutes before saying, "Show me you actually got the gold and you got yourself a deal."

LORI'S GHOST

———————

When Slick went to get the gold, Lori came in and sat down in Johnny's lap. Lori put her arms around Johnny and started to kiss his neck. One of her kisses turned into a bite as she bit a big plug out of Johnny's neck. Johnny jumped up, dumping her on the floor and giving her several kicks for good measure. He squalled, "What the hell is wrong with you? Are you crazy?" Lori sat in the floor, her teeth red with blood, slowly chewing on a piece of Johnny's neck and giggling. Her giggles escalated to ear-splitting cackles.

Slick was back with the sack of gold and, as he looked on, Johnny held a kerchief to his bleeding neck, pulled his pistol and put a bullet between Lori's eyes. She kicked and thrashed around as she made some frightening sounds that were hair-raising to human ears. Lori's whole body quivered as her feet fluttered a rapid beat on the floor before she finally succumbed to death.

Johnny had heard tales about Slick's crazy girlfriend. He pointed his gun at Slick because he didn't know how Slick was going to react to Johnny killing his girlfriend.

Johnny was surprised to see a look of relief on Slick's face. Slick said, "Now, don't go gittin' any big idees. I ain't payin' you no extra for killin' her!"

Slick then turned to One-eye and ordered, "Git some of the boys and go bury her, but I want her buried at least ten miles from here. Also, I want you to dig her grave ten feet deep. Then cover her with two feet of rock, then two feet of dirt, then rock, then dirt, till you git the hole filled up. I don't want her gittin' no crazy notion bout commin' back to visit me."

Slick began to jump at shadows and strange noises. He even had one of the boys sleep in the same room with him at night. None of the hardened outlaws thought any less of Slick. Lori spooked them too, in life and in death.

One night a shot rang out in the camp. When Slick got there, he found Red Irving standing over the body of "Cornbread" Sanders, with a smoking gun still in his hand. Slick asked, "Red, why the hell did you shoot ol' Cornbread?"

By then every man in camp was gathered around. Red replied, "Dammit, I didn't mean to... I heared this noise and saw this shadow. I thought it was that damn Lori so I shot it... Poor ol Cornbread... I really liked him, too."

Every man in camp including Slick understood. They all had been sleeping with their pistols under their pillows.

Johnny went back to the Texican Saloon in Austin. He immediately started trying to prod Jake into a gunfight by announcing to one and all, "Everybody says Jake Jackson is the boar coon in Texas. That's just so much cow shit. The truth is Jake Jackson has been dodging Johnny Concho for years! He is scared to face me. Jackson's got a yellow streak down his back a foot wide. If he ain't yellow, let me come and face me, man to man."

One of the cowhands from Willow Creek was in Austin and heard the loud boasts of Johnny. Upon his return to the ranch, he told the General what Concho was saying about Jake.

Jake was in the bunkhouse. The rustling had dried up but he still patrolled the ranch. Slick had abandoned his efforts to steal the General's cattle until Johnny settled Jake's hash.

The General reluctantly told Jake what Johnny was saying. Jake never blinked or commented other than to say, "I'll be leaving in the morning to go to Austin." Later that night after supper and under a full moon, Jake went outside to scratch Hellfire's neck. Allison had been watching for him. She approached Jake and said, "Jake, no one wants Slick and his gang eliminated more than me. If I could, I'd kill them all myself. But this business with Johnny Concho scares me. I don't know what I'd do if anything happened to you." With that Allison kissed Jake on the lips. Jake's eyes went wide, then he kissed her back. He had not kissed another woman since Macy Kathleen those many years ago.

After a few minutes Jake said, "Allison, you know I'm old enough to be your pa. There cannot be anything between the two of us."

The kiss took Allison's breath away. Her whole body tingled. When she regained her composure, she whispered, "I don't care how old you are. I only care about how I feel. I have never known a man like you. I could never feel about another man the way I feel about you." Jake didn't say anything else, but he squeezed her hand before he went back to the bunk house.

When Jake left at daylight, Allison was watching from her bedroom window. Tears rolled down her face as she prayed, "Dear God, please keep Jake safe and bring him back to me."

HAUNTED
REVENGE

J ake didn't waste any time. As soon as he got to Austin, he went straight to the Texican Saloon. Jake pushed through the swinging doors and immediately stepped to one side. He didn't want to be silhouetted against the door opening while his eyes adjusted to the dim, smoke-filled bar.

Johnny was seated at a corner table, fondling a bar girl who was sitting in his lap. Johnny saw Jake and pushed her off his lap. Jake stepped away from the wall and said, "Concho, I heard that you've been looking for me. Well, here I am."

Johnny slowly stood to his feet. "I have to say, Jackson, I'm surprised to see you. I figured you was yellow. Do you want a last drink fore you die?"

Jake responded, "Is your plan to talk me to death?"

Johnny Concho was fast, real fast. The fastest that Jake had ever seen. Both men got off two shots before the gunfight was over. Johnny's two shots caught Jake in the lower part of his left arm and creased his left thigh. Jake's two shot were a direct hit to the center of Johnny's heart and through his right eye. The slug through his eye blew out the back of Johnny's skull.

Jake immediately turned on his heels, walked out of the saloon without saying another word, leapt on Hellfire's back and started the ride back to Willow Creek. In just a few hours the legendary showdown between Jake Jackson and Johnny Concho was all over Austin. In a few weeks, everybody in Texas was talking about it. Down through the years, so many claimed to have been an eyewitness to the gunfight, there would have to have been over a thousand people crammed into the small bar. The legend of Jake Jackson grew with each retelling of the famous gunfight.

The General and Allison were sitting on the front porch when Jake rode into view. Tears of joy streamed down Allison's face when she saw Jake was returning. Jake had tied up the bullet wound in his arm with a bandana.

When Allison saw his blood stained shirt and pants, her tears turned from joy to concern. Jake slid off Hellfire's back and Allison embraced him. "Jake, are you all right?"

Jake looked at the General to see his reaction at his young daughter embracing the old gunfighter. The General appeared to be taking it well. Jake hugged Allison. "I'm fine. It's just a couple of scratches."

After supper that night, Jake told the General and Allison, "I'm going to be leaving at daylight. It's time to clean out that nest of snakes once and for all." Allison pleaded for Jake not to go, but to no avail. Jake had made up his mind.

The next morning at daylight, the General and Allison were shocked to see Jake mount Hellfire, dressed in just a beech cloth and moccasins with his face painted black for war. They knew Jake Jackson. This was their first introduction to White Wolf, Comanche warrior. He was going to settle this the Comanche way.

Jake knew where the outlaws' camp was as he had previously trailed them there. He left Hellfire in a grove of live oaks and slipped up to a small ridge overlooking the camp. Jake was in no hurry to dispense justice. He wanted the outlaw gang—especially Slick King—to feel the full weight of their actions. Jake wanted them to pay for Allison's humiliation.

There were twenty-seven men in camp, including Slick. As darkness fell, Jake could see the locations of the three men posted for guard duty. The next morning the gang woke up to discover all three men with their throats cut and their bloody scalps stuffed in their mouths.

Slick excitedly said, "One-eye, you take ten men and find the son of a bitch that did this! Bring him to me alive if you can."

After making huge circles around the camp for six hours trying to cut a trail, One-eye and the men came wearily back to camp. "Sorry boss, we didn't find nary hide nor hair of anybody." Slick ranted, raved and slobbered for over an hour.

That night, Slick doubled the guards from three to six. Even though Slick couldn't sleep and checked on the guards periodically, it was almost dawn before he found all six guards with their throats slit, scalped and this time with their genitals stuffed in their mouths.

One-eye spoke first, "How did whoever the hell did this come and go without us seein' or hearin' him?"

Slick was livid with anger. "Damned if I know! I was awake all night checking on them and I didn't see nothing!"

A look of horror came across One-eye's face, "You don't suppose it's that damn Lori?"

Slick swallowed hard, "Not iffen you buried her like I told you!" Slick and the rest of the men thought it might be possible it was her. Slick added, "It's more likely Jake Jackson."

One-eye said in a low voice, "I speck I'd rather have Jackson after me than Lori."

Slick, One-eye and sixteen other gang members were left. Slick took eight and One-eye took eight and went separate ways. They scoured the countryside but found no trace of Jake or Hellfire. That night they sat around the campfire as eighteen pairs of eyes warily searched the darkness.

Suddenly a fierce Comanche war whoop split the silence. Jake and Hellfire streaked through the light from the campfire with Hellfire's belly not far off the ground as he was in a dead sprint. Jake was shooting arrows from his back. The outlaws all pulled their guns and began wildly firing.

Finally Slick shouted, "Quit yer shootin'! Ain't nobody to shoot at!" When the chaos settled down, there were three men dead from arrows and another two from gunshots. The outlaws had accidentally gunned down two of their own.

One of the terrified men exclaimed, "I knew it was that damn Lori! Did you see her face? It looked like a demon from Hell."

Slick answered, "It wasn't Lori, you idjit! It was that damn Jake Jackson! He's gone Comanche on us."

That only left thirteen members of Slick's gang. Three of the men started saddling their horses.

Slick said, "Just where the hell do you think you're goin'?"

One of the men said, "I don't know, but I do know that we gittin' out of here!"

Slick replied, "No you ain't. Nobody leaves unless I say so. We has to stick together."

Another of the three men retorted, "Slick, you can kiss my ass. I'm gone!"

Slick pulled his gun and shot all three men in the back as they started to ride away. "Like I said, ain't nobody goin' nowhere unless I say."

The men huddled around the campfire. Arrows whistled through the air from out of the darkness and thumped home as they found their targets. Two more of Slick's men died with Comanche arrows in their guts. Slick shouted as he started kicking the logs out of the fire, "Put out the damn fire!"

The rest of the men helped him stomp out the fire. The cloud cover blotted out all light from the night sky. The inky blackness horrified the men even more than being exposed by the campfire.

Silent as a shadow, Jake managed to cut two more throats. Jake had learned how to maximize his night vision as a young warrior.

Slick learned of their deaths when they didn't answer a roll call from One-eye. Slick yelled, "Come out and fight like a man, Jackson! You're a damn yellow coward!" Total silence was the only reply Slick got.

Muzzle flashes lit up the night as gunfire erupted. Four of the remaining men died in their own crossfire. Then there was a single gunshot. One-eye could no longer take the pressure and had pressed the end of his barrel to his temple and blew his own brains out. This was the last of Slick's gang. Slick was the only one left.

Slick was curled up in a fetal ball, whimpering. An iron grip pulled him to his feet and Jake whispered in his ear, "Say howdy to Lori for me." Slick gurgled his last breath as blood poured from the knife wound to his throat.

The General and Allison were apprehensive as the Comanche warrior road up to the front porch. Jake noticed that Allison wasn't as eager to hug White Wolf as she had Jake Jackson.

Jake spoke, "General, Slick King and his gang won't be rustling any more of your cattle. My job is done."

The General responded, "Jake, I can't thank you enough for what you've done for us. If I can ever do anything for you, please let me know."

Jake replied. "I will be leaving tomorrow for North Texas. The government is getting close to dissolving the Comanche reservation. I need to be there to help my people make their way in the white world."

Allison didn't try to talk Jake out of leaving. While she was in love with Jake, White Wolf was another matter. Merry old England and their predictable men were beginning to look better and better.

On the ride back to North Texas, Jake knew there was no going back to being only Comanche. He was now and forever part of the white world. But in his heart Jake longed for the days when he was only Comanche. He would always hold dear to his heart the Comanche way.

EPILOGUE

In his later years, Quanah Parker was asked his view on religion. His reply became famous: "The white man goes into his church and talks about Jesus. The Indian goes into his tipi and talks with Jesus."

ACKNOWLEDGEMENTS

I am grateful for the constant support of my wife, Tina, and my children: Jacob, Caleb, Sarah and Ainslee.

Thank you to Missy Brewer for editing this book, to Michael Campbell for the book design, and to Bryan Gehrke for the cover artwork.

William Joiner can be contacted at bridgetexas@yahoo.com

*Jesus answered, "I am the way
and the truth and the life.
No one comes to the Father
except through me."*

— JOHN 14:6

44814117R00113

Made in the USA
Charleston, SC
09 August 2015